HARPERCOLLINS CHILDREN'S

Stories
for

Year Olds

In the same series:

HARPERCOLLINS CHILDREN'S

Stories for

Year Olds

Compiled by Julia Eccleshare

HarperCollins *Children's Books*

First published in the United Kingdom by HarperCollins, Young Lions, in 1992
Published in this revised edition by HarperCollins *Children's Books* in 2022
HarperCollins *Children's Books* is a division of HarperCollins*Publishers* Ltd
1 London Bridge Street
London SE1 9GF

www.harpercollins.co.uk

HarperCollins*Publishers*
1st Floor, Watermarque Building, Ringsend Road
Dublin 4, Ireland

1

ISBN 978-0-00-852476-0

A CIP catalogue record for this title is available from the British Library.

Typeset in 13/24pt ITC Century Std by Palimpsest Book Production Ltd,
Falkirk, Stirlingshire

Printed and bound in the UK using 100% renewable electricity at CPI Group (UK) Ltd

Contents

The Silver Swan

Michael Morpurgo
Illustrated by Ruthine Burton

*T*he silver swan, who living had no note,
  When death approached, unlocked her
silent throat:
Leaning her breast against the reedy shore
Thus sung her first and last, and sung no more.

Orlando Gibbons

A swan came to my loch one day, a silver swan. I was fishing for trout in the moonlight.

She came flying in above me, her wings singing in the air. She circled the loch twice, and then landed, silver, silver in the moonlight.

I stood and watched her as she arranged her wings behind her and sailed out over the loch, making it entirely her own. I stayed as late as I could, quite unable to leave her.

I went down to the loch every day after that, but not to fish for trout, simply to watch my silver swan.

In those early days I took great care not to frighten her away, keeping myself still and hidden in the shadow of the alders. But even so, she knew I was there – I was sure of it.

Within a week I would find her cruising along the lochside, waiting for me when I arrived in the early mornings. I took to bringing some bread crusts with me. She would look sideways at them at first, rather disdainfully. Then, after a while, she reached out her neck, snatched them out of the water, and made off with them in triumph.

One day I dared to dunk the bread crusts for her, dared to try to feed her by hand. She took all I offered her and came back for more. She was coming close enough now for me to be able to touch her neck. I would talk to her as I stroked her. She really listened, I know she did.

I never saw the cob arrive. He was just there swimming beside her one morning out on the loch. You could see the love between

11

them even then. The princess of the loch had found her prince. When they drank they dipped their necks together, as one. When they flew, their wings beat together, as one.

She knew I was there, I think, still watching. But she did not come to see me again, nor to have her bread crusts. I tried to be more glad for her than sad for me, but it was hard.

As winter tried, and failed, to turn to spring, they began to make a home on the small island, way out in the middle of the loch. I could watch them now only through my binoculars. I was there every day I could be – no matter what the weather.

Things were happening. They were no longer busy just preening themselves, or feeding, or simply gliding out over the loch taking their reflections with them. Between them they were building a nest – a clumsy messy excuse for a nest it seemed to me – set on a reedy knoll near the shore of their island.

It took them several days to construct. Neither ever seemed quite satisfied with the other's work. A twig was too big, or too small, or perhaps just not in the right place. There were no arguments as such, as far as I could see. But my silver swan would rearrange things, tactfully, when her cob wasn't there. And he would do the same when she wasn't there.

Then, one bright cold morning with the ground beneath my feet hard with a late and unexpected frost, I arrived to see my silver swan enthroned at last on her nest, her cob proudly patrolling the loch close by.

I knew there were foxes about even then. I had heard their cries often enough echoing through the night. I had seen their footprints in the snow. But I had never seen one out and about, until now.

It was dusk. I was on my way back home from the loch, coming up through the woods, when I spotted a family of five cubs, their mother sitting on guard nearby. Unseen and unsmelt, I crouched down where I was and watched.

I could see at once that they were starving, some of them already too weak even to pester their mother for food. But I could see too that she had none to give – she was thin and rangy herself. I remember thinking then: *That's one family of foxes that's not likely to make it, not if the spring doesn't come soon, not if this winter goes on much longer.*

But the winter did go on that year, on and on.

I thought little more of the foxes. My mind was on other things, more important things. My silver swan and her cob shared the sitting duties and the guarding duties, never leaving the precious nest long enough for me even to catch sight of the eggs, let alone count them. But I could count the days, and I did.

As the day approached I made up my mind I would go down to the loch, no matter what, and stay there until it happened – however long that might take. But the great day dawned foggy. Out of my bedroom window, I could barely see across the farmyard.

I ran all the way down to the loch. From the lochside I could see nothing of the island, nothing of the loch, only a few feet of limpid grey water lapping at the muddy shore. I could hear the muffled *aarking* of a heron out in the fog, and the distant piping of a moorhen. But I stayed to keep watch, all that day, all the next.

I was there in the morning two days later when the fog began at last to lift and the pale sun began to come through. The island was there again. I turned my binoculars at once on the nest. It was deserted. They were gone. I scanned the loch, still mist-covered in places. Not a ripple. Nothing.

Then out of nothing they appeared, my silver swan, her cob and four cygnets, coming straight towards me. As they came towards

the shore they turned and sailed right past me. I swear she was showing them to me, parading them. They both swam with such easy power, the cygnets bobbing along in their wake. But I had counted wrong. There was another one, hitching a ride in among his mother's folded wings. A snug little swan, I thought, littler than the others perhaps. A lucky little swan.

That night the wind came in from the north and the loch froze over. It stayed frozen. I wondered how they would manage. But I need not have worried. They swam about, keeping a pool of water near the island clear of ice. They had enough to eat, enough to drink. They would be fine. And every day the cygnets were growing. It was clear now that one of them was indeed much smaller, much weaker. But he was keeping up. He was coping. All was well.

Then, silently, as I slept one night, it snowed outside. It snowed on the farm, on the trees, on the frozen loch. I took bread crusts with me the next morning, just in case, and hurried down to the loch. As I came out of the woods I saw the fox's paw prints in the snow. They were leading down towards the loch.

I was running, stumbling through the drifts, dreading all along what I might find.

The fox was stalking around the nest. My silver swan was standing her ground over her young, neck lowered in attack, her wings beating the air frantically, furiously. I shouted. I screamed. But I was too late and too far away to help.

Quick as a flash the fox darted in, had her by the wing and was dragging her away. I ran out on to the ice. I felt it crack and give suddenly beneath me. I was knee-deep in the loch then, still screaming, but the fox would not be put off. I could see the blood, red, bright red, on the snow.

The five cygnets were scattering in their terror. My silver swan was still fighting. But she was losing, and there was nothing I could do.

I heard the sudden singing of wings above me. The cob! The cob flying in, diving to attack. The fox took one look upwards, released her victim, and scampered off over the ice, chased all the way by the cob.

For some moments I thought my silver swan was dead. She lay so still on the snow.

But then she was on her feet and limping back to her island, one wing flapping feebly, the other trailing, covered in blood and useless. She was gathering her cygnets about her. They were all there. She was enfolding them, loving them, when the cob came flying back to her, landing awkwardly on the ice.

He stood over her all that day and would not leave her side. He knew she was dying. So, by then, did I. I had nothing but revenge and murder in my heart. Time and again, as I sat there at the lochside, I thought of taking my father's gun and going into the woods to hunt down the killer fox. But then I would think of her cubs and would know that she was only doing what a mother fox had to do.

For days I kept my cold sad vigil by the

loch. The cob was sheltering the cygnets now, my silver swan sleeping nearby, her head tucked under her wing. She scarcely ever moved.

I wasn't there, but I knew the precise moment she died. I knew it because she sang it. It's quite true what they say about swans singing only when they die. I was at home. I had been sent out to fetch logs for the fire before I went up to bed. The world about me was crisp and bright under the moon. The song was clearer and sweeter than any human voice, than any birdsong, I had ever heard before. So sang my silver swan and died.

I expected to see her lying dead on the island the next morning. But she was not there. The cob was sitting still as a statue on his nest, his five cygnets around him.

I went looking for her. I picked up the trail of feathers and blood at the lochside, and followed where I knew it must lead, up through the woods. I approached silently. The fox cubs were frolicking fat and furry in the sunshine, their mother close by intent on her grooming. There was a terrible wreath of white feathers nearby, and tell-tale feathers too on her snout. She was trying to shake them off. How I hated her.

I ran at her. I picked up stones. I hurled them. I screamed at her. The foxes vanished into the undergrowth and left me alone in the woods. I picked up a silver feather, and cried tears of such raw grief, such fierce anger.

Spring came at long last the next day, and melted the ice. The cob and his five cygnets were safe. After that I came less and less to the loch. It wasn't quite the same without my silver swan. I went there only now and again, just to see how he was doing, how they were all doing.

At first, to my great relief, it seemed as if he was managing well enough on his own. Then one day I noticed there were only four cygnets swimming alongside him, the four bigger ones. I don't know what happened to the smaller one. He just wasn't there. Not so lucky, after all.

The cob would sometimes bring his cygnets to the lochside to see me. I would feed them when he came, but then after a while he just stopped coming.

The weeks passed and the months passed, and the cygnets grew and flew. The cob scarcely left his island now. He stayed on the very spot I had last seen my silver swan. He did not swim; he did not feed; he did not preen himself. Day by day it became clearer that he was pining for her, dying for her.

Now my vigil at the lochside was almost constant again. I had to be with him; I had to see him through. It was what my silver swan would have wanted, I thought.

So I was there when it happened. A swan flew in from nowhere one day, down on to the glassy stillness of the loch. She landed right in front of him. He walked down into the loch, settled into the water and swam out to meet her. I watched them look each other over for just a few minutes. When they drank, they dipped their necks together, as one. When they flew, their wings beat together, as one.

Five years on and they're still together. Five years on and I still have the feather from my silver swan. I take it with me wherever I go. I always will.

Mary Poppins Comes Back:
Topsy Turvy

P. L. Travers
Illustrated by Mary Shephard

'Keep close to me, please!' said Mary
Poppins, stepping out of the bus and
putting up her umbrella, for it was raining
heavily.

Jane and Michael scrambled out after her.

'If I keep close to you the drips from your umbrella run down my neck,' complained Michael.

'Don't blame me, then, if you get lost and have to ask a Policeman!' snapped Mary Poppins, as she neatly avoided a puddle.

She paused outside the Chemist's shop at the corner so that she could see herself reflected in the three gigantic bottles in the window. She could see a Green Mary Poppins, a Blue Mary Poppins and a Red Mary Poppins all at once. And each one of them was carrying a brand-new leather handbag with brass knobs on it.

Mary Poppins looked at herself in the three bottles and smiled a pleased and satisfied smile. She spent some minutes changing the handbag from her right hand to her left, trying it in every possible position to see how it looked best. Then she decided that, after all, it was most effective when tucked under her arm. So she left it there.

Jane and Michael stood beside her, not daring to say anything but glancing across at each other and sighing inside themselves. And from two points of her parrot-handled umbrella the rain trickled uncomfortably down the backs of their necks.

'Now then – don't keep me waiting!' said Mary Poppins crossly, turning away from the Green, Blue and Red reflections of herself. Jane and Michael exchanged glances. Jane signalled to Michael to keep quiet. She shook her head and made a face at him. But he burst out: 'We weren't. It was you keeping us waiting—!'

'Silence!'

Michael did not dare to say any more. He and Jane trudged along, one on either side of Mary Poppins. The rain poured down, dancing from the top of the umbrella on to their hats. Under her arm Jane carried the Royal Doulton Bowl wrapped carefully in two pieces of paper. They were taking it to Mary Poppins' cousin, Mr Turvy, whose business, she told Mrs Banks, was mending things.

'Well,' Mrs Banks had said, rather doubtfully, 'I hope he will do it satisfactorily, for until it *is* mended I shall not be able to look my Great-Aunt Caroline in the face.'

Great-Aunt Caroline had given Mrs Banks the bowl when Mrs Banks was only three, and it was well known that if it were broken Great-

Aunt Caroline would make one of her famous scenes.

'Members of *my* family, ma'am,' Mary Poppins had retorted with a sniff, *'always give satisfaction.'*

And she had looked so fierce that Mrs Banks felt quite uncomfortable and had to sit down and ring for a cup of tea.

Swish!

There was Jane, right in the middle of a puddle.

'Look where you're going, please!' snapped Mary Poppins, shaking her umbrella and tossing the drips over Jane and Michael. 'This rain is enough to break your heart.'

'If it did, could Mr Turvy mend it?' enquired Michael. He was interested to know if Mr

Turvy could mend all broken things or only certain kinds.

'One more word,' said Mary Poppins, 'and Back Home you go!'

'I only asked,' said Michael sulkily.

'Then don't!'

Mary Poppins, with an angry sniff, turned the corner smartly and, opening an old iron gate, knocked at the door of a small tumble-down building.

'Tap-tap-tappity-tap!' The sound of the knocker echoed hollowly through the house.

'Oh, dear,' Jane whispered to Michael, 'how awful if he's out!' But at that moment heavy footsteps were heard tramping towards them, and with a loud rattle the door opened.

A round, red-faced woman, looking more like two apples placed one on top of the other

than a human being, stood in the doorway.
Her straight hair was scraped into a knob at
the top of her head, and her thin mouth had
a cross and peevish expression.

'Well!' she said, staring. 'It's you or I'm a
Dutchman!' She did not seem particularly
pleased to see Mary Poppins. Nor did Mary
Poppins seem particularly pleased to see
her.

'Is Mr Turvy in?' she enquired, without
taking any notice of the woman's remark.

'Well,' said the round woman in an unfriendly
voice, 'I wouldn't be certain. He may be or he
may not. It's all a matter of how you happen
to look at it.'

Mary Poppins stepped through the door and
peered about her.

'That's his hat, isn't it?' she demanded,

pointing to an old felt hat that hung on a peg in the hall.

'Well, it is, of course – in a manner of speaking.' The round woman admitted the fact unwillingly.

'Then he's in,' said Mary Poppins. 'No member of *my* family ever goes out without a hat. They're much too respectable.'

'Well, all I can tell you is what he said to me this morning,' said the round woman. "Miss Tartlet,' he said, 'I may be in this afternoon and I may not. It is quite impossible to tell.' That's what he said. But you'd better go up and see for yourself. I'm not a Mountaineer.'

The round woman glanced down at her round body and Mary Poppins shook her head. Jane and Michael could easily understand that a person of her size and shape would not want

to climb Mr Turvy's narrow, rickety stairs very often.

Mary Poppins sniffed.

'Follow me, please!' She snapped the words at Jane and Michael, and they ran after her up the creaking stairs. Miss Tartlet stood in the hall watching them with a superior smile on her face.

At the top landing Mary Poppins knocked on the door with the head of the umbrella. There was no reply. She knocked again – louder this time. Still there was no answer.

'Cousin Arthur!' she called through the keyhole. 'Cousin Arthur, are you in?'

'No, I'm out!' came a faraway voice from within.

'How can he be out? I can hear him!' whispered Michael to Jane.

'Cousin Arthur!' Mary Poppins rattled the door handle. 'I know you're in.'

'No, no, I'm not!' came the faraway voice. 'I'm out, I tell you. It's the Second Monday!'

'Oh, dear – I'd forgotten!' said Mary Poppins, and with an angry movement she turned the handle and flung open the door.

At first, all that Jane and Michael could see was a large room that appeared to be quite empty except for a carpenter's bench at one end. Piled upon this was a curious collection of articles – china dogs with no noses, wooden horses that had lost their tails, chipped plates, broken dolls, knives without handles, stools with only two legs – everything in the world, it seemed, that could possibly want mending.

Round the walls of the room were shelves

reaching from floor to ceiling and these, too, were crowded with cracked china, broken glass and shattered toys.

But there was no sign anywhere of a human being.

'Oh,' said Jane in a disappointed voice. 'He *is* out, after all!'

But Mary Poppins had darted across the room to the window.

'Come in at once, Arthur! Out in the rain like that, and you with your Bronchitis the winter before last!'

And, to their amazement, Jane and Michael saw her grasp a long leg that hung across the windowsill and pull in from the outer air a tall, thin, sad-looking man with a long, drooping moustache.

'You ought to be ashamed of yourself,' said

Mary Poppins crossly, keeping a firm hold of Mr Turvy with one hand while she shut the window with the other. 'We've brought you some important work to do and here you are behaving like this!'

'Well, I can't help it,' said Mr Turvy apologetically, mopping his sad eyes with a large handkerchief. 'I told you it was the Second Monday.'

'What does that mean?' asked Michael, staring at Mr Turvy with interest.

'Ah,' said Mr Turvy, turning to him and shaking him limply by the hand. 'It's kind of you to inquire, very kind. I do appreciate it, really.' He paused to wipe his eyes again. 'You see,' he went on, 'it's this way. On the Second Monday of the month everything goes wrong with me.'

'What kind of things?' asked Jane, feeling very sorry for Mr Turvy, but also very curious.

'Well, take today!' said Mr Turvy. 'This happens to be the Second Monday of the month. And because I want to be in – having so much work to do – I'm automatically out. And if I wanted to be out, sure enough, I'd be in.'

'I see,' said Jane, though she really found it very difficult to understand. 'So that's why—?'

'Yes.' Mr Turvy nodded. 'I heard you coming up the stairs and I did so long to be in. So, of course, as soon as that happened – there I was – out! And I'd be out still if Mary Poppins weren't holding on to me.' He sighed heavily.

'Of course, it's not like this all the time. Only between the hours of three and six – but even then it can be very awkward.'

'I'm sure it can,' said Jane sympathetically.

'And it's not as if it was only In and Out,' Mr Turvy went on miserably. 'It's other things too. If I try to go upstairs, I find myself running down. I have only to turn to the right and I find myself going to the left. And I never set off for the West without immediately finding myself in the East.'

Mr Turvy blew his nose.

'And worst of all,' he continued, his eyes filling again with tears, 'my whole nature alters. To look at me now, you'd hardly believe I was really a happy and satisfied sort of person – would you?'

And, indeed, Mr Turvy looked so melancholy and distressed that it seemed quite impossible he could ever have been cheerful and contented.

'But, why? Why?' demanded Michael, staring up at him.

Mr Turvy shook his head sadly.

'Ah!' he said solemnly. 'I should have been a Girl.'

Jane and Michael stared at him and then at each other. What *could* he mean?

'You see,' Mr Turvy explained, 'my Mother wanted a girl, and it turned out, when I arrived, that I was a boy. So I went wrong right from the beginning – from the day I was born, you might say. And that was the Second Monday of the month.'

Mr Turvy began to weep again, sobbing gently into his handkerchief.

Jane patted his hand kindly.

He seemed pleased, though he did not smile.

'And, of course,' he went on, 'it's very bad for my work. Look up there!'

He pointed to one of the larger shelves, on which were standing a row of hearts in different colours and sizes, each one cracked or chipped or entirely broken.

'Now, those,' said Mr Turvy, 'are wanted in a great hurry. You don't know how cross people get if I don't send their hearts back quickly. They make more fuss about them than anything else. And I simply daren't touch them till after six o'clock. They'd be ruined – like those things!'

He nodded to another shelf. Jane and Michael looked and saw that it was piled high with things that had been wrongly mended. A china Shepherdess had been separated from her china Shepherd and her arms were glued about the neck of a brass Lion; a Toy Sailor, whom somebody had wrenched from his boat, was firmly stuck to a Willow-pattern plate; and in the boat, with his trunk curled round the mast and fixed there with sticking-plaster, was a grey-flannel Elephant. Broken saucers were riveted together the wrong way of the pattern, and the leg of a wooden Horse was firmly attached to a silver Christening Mug.

'You see?' said Mr Turvy hopelessly, with a wave of his hand.

Jane and Michael nodded. They felt very, very sorry for Mr Turvy.

'Well, never mind that now,' Mary Poppins broke in impatiently. 'What *is* important is this Bowl. We've brought it to be mended.'

She took the Bowl from Jane and, still holding Mr Turvy with one hand, she untied the string with the other.

'Hm!' said Mr Turvy. 'Royal Doulton. A bad crack. Looks as though somebody had thrown something at it.'

Jane felt herself blushing as he said that.

'Still,' he went on, 'if it were any other day, I could mend it. But today—' he hesitated.

'Nonsense, it's quite simple. You've only to put a rivet here – and here – and here!'

Mary Poppins pointed to the crack, and, as she did so, she dropped Mr Turvy's hand.

Immediately, he went spinning through the air, turning over and over like a Catherine wheel.

'Oh!' cried Mr Turvy. 'Why did you let go? Poor me, I'm off again!'

'Quick – shut the door!' cried Mary Poppins. And Jane and Michael rushed across the room and closed the door just before Mr Turvy reached it. He banged against it and bounced away again, turning gracefully, with a very sad look on his face, through the air.

Suddenly he stopped, but in a very curious position. Instead of being right-side-up he was upside down and standing on his head.

'Dear, dear!' said Mr Turvy, giving a fierce kick with his feet. 'Dear, dear!'

But his feet would not go down to the floor. They remained waving gently in the air.

'Well,' Mr Turvy remarked in his melancholy voice, 'I suppose I should be glad it's no worse. This is certainly better – though not *much* better – than hanging outside in the rain with nothing to sit on and no overcoat.

46

You see,' he looked at Jane and Michael, 'I want so much to be right-side-up and so – just my luck! – I'm upside down. Well, well, never mind. I ought to be used to it by now. I've had forty-five years of it. Give me the Bowl.'

Michael ran and took the Bowl from Mary Poppins and put it on the floor by Mr Turvy's head. And, as he did so, he felt a curious thing happening to him. The floor seemed to be pushing his feet away from it and tilting them into the air. 'Oh!' he cried. 'I feel so funny. Something most extraordinary is happening to me!'

For by now, he, too, was turning Catherine wheels through the air, and flying up and down the room, until he landed head-first on the floor beside Mr Turvy.

'Strike me pink!' said Mr Turvy in a surprised

voice, looking at Michael out of the corner of his eye. 'I never knew it was catching. You too? Well, of all the – Hi, Hi, I say! Steady there! You'll knock the goods off the shelves, if you're not careful, and I shall be charged for breakages. What *are* you doing?'

He was now addressing Jane, whose feet had suddenly swept off the carpet and were turning above her head in the giddiest manner. Over and over she went – first her head and then her feet in the air – until at last she came down on the other side of Mr Turvy and found herself standing on her head.

'You know,' said Mr Turvy, staring at her solemnly, 'this is very odd. I never knew it happen to anyone else before. Upon my word, I never did. I do hope you don't mind.'

Jane laughed, turning her head towards him and waving her legs in the air.

'Not a bit, thank you. I've always wanted to stand on my head and I've never been able to do it before. It's very comfortable.'

'Hm,' said Mr Turvy dolefully. 'I'm glad somebody likes it. I can't say *I* feel like that.'

'I do,' said Michael. 'I wish I could stay like this all my life. Everything looks so nice and different.'

And, indeed, everything *was* different. From their strange position on the floor, Jane and Michael could see that the articles on the carpenter's bench were all upside down – china dogs, broken dolls, wooden stools – all standing on their heads.

'Look!' whispered Jane to Michael. He turned his head as much as he could. And there, creeping out of a hole in the wainscoting, came a small mouse. It skipped, head over heels, into the middle of the room, and, turning upside down, balanced daintily on its nose in front of them.

They watched it for a moment, very surprised. Then Michael suddenly said: 'Jane, look out of the window!'

She turned her head carefully, for it was rather difficult, and saw to her astonishment that everything outside the room, as well as everything in it, was different. Out in the street the houses were standing on their heads, their chimneys on the pavement and their doorsteps in the air, and out of the doorsteps came little curls of smoke. In the distance a church had turned turtle and was balancing rather top-heavily on the point of its steeple. And the rain, which had always seemed to them to come down from the sky, was pouring up from the earth in a steady, soaking shower.

'Oh,' said Jane, 'how beautifully strange it all is! It's like being in another world. I'm so glad we came today.'

'Well,' said Mr Turvy mournfully, 'you're very kind, I must say. You do know how to make allowances. Now, what about this Bowl?'

He stretched out his hand to take it, but at that moment the Bowl gave a little skip and turned upside down. And it did it so quickly and so funnily that Jane and Michael could not help laughing.

'This,' said Mr Turvy miserably, 'is no

laughing matter for me, I assure you. I shall have to put the rivets in wrong way up – and if they show, they show. I can't help it.' And, taking his tools out of his pocket, he mended the Bowl, weeping quietly as he worked.

'Humph!' said Mary Poppins, stooping to pick it up. 'Well, that's done. And now we'll be going.'

At that Mr Turvy began to sob pitifully.

'That's right, leave me!' he said bitterly. 'Don't stay and help me keep my mind off my misery. Don't hold out a friendly hand. I'm not worth it. I'd hoped you might all favour me by accepting some refreshment. There's a Plum Cake in a tin on the top shelf. But, there – I'd no right to expect it. You've your own lives to live and I shouldn't ask you to stay and brighten mine. This isn't my lucky day.'

He fumbled for his pocket handkerchief.

'Well—' began Mary Poppins, pausing in the middle of buttoning her gloves.

'Oh, do stay, Mary Poppins, do!' cried Jane and Michael together, dancing eagerly on their heads.

'You could reach the cake if you stood on a chair!' said Jane helpfully.

Mr Turvy laughed for the first time. It was rather a melancholy sound, but still, it *was* a laugh.

'*She'll* need no chair!' he said gloomily, chuckling in his throat. 'She'll get what she wants and in the way she wants it – *she* will.'

And at that moment, before the children's astonished eyes, Mary Poppins did a curious thing. She raised herself stiffly on her toes and balanced there for a moment. Then, very slowly, and in a most dignified manner, she turned seven Catherine wheels through the air. Over and over, her skirts clinging neatly about her ankles, her hat set tidily on her head, she wheeled up to the top shelf, took the cake, and wheeled down again, landing neatly on her head in front of Mr Turvy and the children.

'Hooray! Hooray! Hooray!' shouted Michael delightedly. But from the floor Mary Poppins gave him such a look that he rather wished he had remained silent.

'Thank you, Mary,' said Mr Turvy sadly, not seeming at all surprised.

'There!' snapped Mary Poppins. 'That's the last thing I do for you today.'

She put the cake-tin down in front of Mr Turvy.

Immediately, with a little wobbly roll, it turned upside down. And each time Mr Turvy turned it right-side-up, it turned over again.

'Ah,' he said despairingly, 'I might have known it. Nothing is right today – not even the cake-tin. We shall have to cut it open from the bottom. I'll just ask—'

And he stumbled on his head to the door and shouted through the crack between it and the floor.

'Miss Tartlet! Miss Tartlet! I'm so sorry to trouble you, but could you – would you – do you mind bringing a tin-opener?'

Far away downstairs Miss Tartlet's voice could be heard, grimly protesting.

'Tush!' said a loud croaky voice inside the room. 'Tush and nonsense! Don't bother the

55

woman! Let Polly do it! Pretty Polly! Clever Polly!'

Turning their heads, Jane and Michael were surprised to see that the voice came from Mary Poppins' parrot-headed umbrella which was at that moment Catherine-wheeling towards the cake. It landed head-downwards on the tin and in two seconds had cut a large hole in it with its beak.

'There!' squawked the parrot-head conceitedly. 'Polly did it! Handsome Polly!' And a happy self-satisfied smile spread over its beak as it settled head-downwards on the floor beside Mary Poppins.

'Well, that's very kind, *very* kind!' said Mr Turvy in his gloomy voice, as the dark crust of the cake became visible.

He took a knife out of his pocket and cut

a slice. He started violently, and peered at the cake more closely. Then he looked reproachfully at Mary Poppins.

'This is your doing, Mary! Don't deny it. That cake, when the tin was last open, was a Plum Cake, and now—'

'Sponge is more digestible,' said Mary Poppins primly.

'Eat slowly, please. You're not Starving Savages!' she snapped, passing a small slice each to Jane and Michael.

'That's all very well,' grumbled Mr Turvy bitterly, eating his slice in two bites. 'But I do like a plum or two, I must admit. Ah, well, this is not my lucky day!' He broke off as somebody rapped loudly on the door.

'Come in!' called Mr Turvy.

Miss Tartlet, looking, if anything, rounder

than ever, and panting from her climb up the stairs, burst into the room.

'The tin-opener, Mr Turvy—' she began grimly. Then she paused and stared.

'My!' she said, opening her mouth very wide and letting the tin-opener slip from her hand. 'Of all the sights I ever did see, this is the one I wouldn't have expected!'

She took a step forward, gazing at the four pairs of waving feet with an expression of deep disgust.

'Upside down – the lot of you – like flies on a ceiling! And you are supposed to be respectable human creatures. This is no place for a lady of *my* standing. I shall leave the house this instant, Mr Turvy. Please note that!'

She flounced angrily towards the door.

But even as she went her great billowing

skirts blew against her round legs and lifted her from the floor.

A look of agonised astonishment spread over her face. She flung out her hands wildly.

'Mr Turvy! Mr Turvy, sir! Catch me! Hold me down! Help! Help!' cried Miss Tartlet, as she, too, began a sweeping Catherine wheel.

'Oh, oh, the world's turning turtle! What shall I do? Help! Help!' she shrieked, as she went over again.

But as she turned, a curious change came over her. Her round face lost its peevish expression and began to shine with smiles. And Jane and Michael, with a start of surprise, saw her straight hair crinkle into a mass of little curls as she whirled and twirled through the room. When she spoke again, her gruff voice was as sweet as honeysuckle.

'What can be happening to me?' cried Miss Tartlet's new voice. 'I feel like a ball! A bouncing ball! Or perhaps a balloon! Or a cherry tart!' She broke into a peal of happy laughter.

'Dear me, how cheerful I am!' she trilled, turning and circling through the air. 'I never enjoyed my life before, but now I feel I shall never stop. It's the loveliest sensation. I shall write home to my Sister about it, to my cousins and uncles and aunts. I shall tell them that the only proper way to live is upside down, upside down, upside down—'

And, chanting happily, Miss Tartlet went whirling round and round. Jane and Michael watched her with delight and Mr Turvy watched her with surprise, for he had never known Miss Tartlet to be anything but peevish and unfriendly.

'Very odd! Very odd!' said Mr Turvy to himself, shaking his head as he stood on it.

Another knock sounded at the door.

'Anyone here name of Turvy?' enquired a voice, and the Post Man appeared in the doorway holding a letter. He stood staring at the sight that met his eyes.

'Holy smoke!' he remarked, pushing his cap to the back of his head. 'I must-a come to the wrong place. I'm looking for a decent, quiet gentleman called Turvy. I've got a letter for him. Besides, I promised my wife I'd be home early and I've broken my word, and I thought—'

'Ha!' said Mr Turvy from the floor. 'A broken promise is one of the things I can't mend. Not in my line. Sorry!'

The Post Man stared down at him.

'Am I dreaming or am I not?' he muttered.

'It seems to me I've got into a whirling, twirling, skirling company of lunatics!'

'Give me the letter, dear Post Man! Mr Turvy, you see, is engaged! Give the letter to Topsy Tartlet and turn upside down with me.'

Miss Tartlet, wheeling towards the Post Man, took his hand in hers. And as she touched him his feet slithered off the floor into the air. Then away they went, hand in hand, and over and over, like a pair of bouncing footballs.

'How lovely it is!' cried Miss Tartlet happily. 'Oh, Post Man, dear, we're seeing life for the first time. And such a pleasant view of it! Over we go! Isn't it wonderful?'

'Yes!' shouted Jane and Michael, as they joined the wheeling dance of the Post Man and Miss Tartlet. Presently Mr Turvy, too, joined in, awkwardly turning and tossing through the air. Mary Poppins and her umbrella followed, going over and over evenly and neatly and with the utmost dignity. There they all were, spinning and wheeling, with the world going up and down outside, and the happy cries of Miss Tartlet echoing through the room.

> *'The whole of the Town*
> *Is Upside Down!'*

she sang, bouncing and bounding.

And up on the shelves the cracked and broken hearts twirled and spun like tops, the Shepherdess and her Lion waltzed gracefully together, the grey-flannel Elephant stood on his trunk in the boat and kicked his feet in the air, and the Toy Sailor danced a hornpipe, not on his feet but his head, which bobbed about the Willow-pattern plate very gracefully.

'How happy I am!' cried Jane, as she careered across the room.

'How happy *I* am!' cried Michael, turning somersaults in the air.

Mr Turvy mopped his eyes with his handkerchief as he bounced off the window-pane.

Mary Poppins and her umbrella said nothing, but just sailed calmly round, head downwards.

'How happy we *all* are!' cried Miss Tartlet.

But the Post Man had now found his tongue and he did not agree with her.

"Ere!' he shouted, turning again. "Elp! 'Elp! Where am I? Who am I? What am I? I don't know at all. I'm lost! Oh, 'elp!'

But nobody helped him and, firmly held

in Miss Tartlet's grasp, he was whirled on.

'Always lived a quiet life – I have!' he moaned. 'Behaved like a decent citizen too. Oh, what'll my wife say? And 'ow shall I get 'ome? 'Elp! Fire! Thieves!'

And, making a great effort, he wrenched his hand violently from Miss Tartlet's. He dropped the letter into the cake-tin and went wheeling out of the door and down the stairs, head over heels, crying loudly:

'I'll have the law on them! I'll call the Police! I'll speak to the Post Master General!'

His voice died away as he went bounding farther down the stairs.

Ping, ping, ping, ping, ping, ping!

The clock outside in the Square sounded six.

And at the same moment Jane's and

Michael's feet came down to the floor with a thud, and they stood up, feeling rather giddy.

Mary Poppins gracefully turned right-side-up, looking as smart and tidy as a figure in a shop window.

The umbrella wheeled over and stood on its point. Mr Turvy, with a great tossing of legs, scrambled to his feet.

The hearts on the shelf stood still and steady, and no movement came from the Shepherdess or the Lion, or the grey-flannel Elephant or the Toy Sailor. To look at them you would never have guessed that a moment before they had all been dancing on their heads.

Only Miss Tartlet went whirling on, round and round the room, feet over head, laughing happily and singing her song.

'The whole of the Town

Is Upside Down,

Upside Down,

Upside Down!'

she chanted joyfully.

'Miss Tartlet! Miss Tartlet!' cried Mr Turvy, running towards her, a strange light in her eyes. He took her arm as she wheeled past and held it tightly until she stood upon her feet beside him.

'*What* did you say your name was?' said Mr Turvy, panting with excitement.

Miss Tartlet actually blushed. She looked at him shyly.

'Why, Tartlet, sir. Topsy Tartlet!'

Mr Turvy took her hand.

'Then will you marry me, Miss Tartlet, and

be Topsy Turvy? It would make up to me for so much. And you seem to have become so happy that perhaps you will be kind enough to overlook my Second Mondays.'

'Overlook them, Mr Turvy? Why, they will be my Greatest Treats,' said Miss Tartlet. 'I have seen the world upside down today and I have got a New Point of View. I assure you I shall look forward to the Second Mondays all the month!'

She laughed shyly, and gave Mr Turvy her other hand. And Mr Turvy, Jane and Michael were glad to see, laughed too.

'It's after six o'clock, so I suppose he can be himself again,' whispered Michael to Jane.

Jane did not answer. She was watching the mouse. It was no longer standing on its nose but hurrying away to its hole with a large crumb of cake in its mouth.

Mary Poppins picked up the Royal Doulton Bowl and proceeded to wrap it up.

'Pick up your handkerchiefs, please – and straighten your hats,' she snapped.

'And now—' She took her umbrella and tucked her new bag under her arm.

'Oh, we're not going yet, are we, Mary Poppins?' said Michael.

'If *you* are in the habit of staying out all night, I am not,' she remarked, pushing him towards the door.

'Must you go, really?' said Mr Turvy. But he seemed to be saying it out of mere politeness. He had eyes only for Miss Tartlet.

But Miss Tartlet herself came up to them, smiling radiantly and tossing her curls.

'Come again,' she said, giving a hand to each of them. 'Now do. Mr Turvy and I –' she looked down shyly and blushed – 'will be in to tea every Second Monday – won't we, Arthur?'

'Well,' said Mr Turvy, 'we'll be in if we're not out – I'm sure of that!'

He and Miss Tartlet stood at the top of the stairs waving goodbye to Mary Poppins and the children – Miss Tartlet blushing happily, and Mr Turvy holding Miss Tartlet's hand and looking very proud and pompous . . .

'I didn't know it was as easy as that,' said Michael to Jane, as they splashed through the rain under Mary Poppins' umbrella.

'What was?' said Jane.

'Standing on my head. I shall practise it when I get home.'

'I wish *we* could have Second Mondays,' said Jane dreamily.

'Get in, please!' said Mary Poppins, shutting her umbrella and pushing the children up the winding stairs of the bus.

They sat together in the seat behind hers, talking quietly about all that had happened that afternoon.

Mary Poppins turned and glared at them.

'It is rude to whisper,' she said fiercely. 'And sit up straight. You're not flour bags!'

They were quiet for a few minutes. Mary Poppins, half turning in her seat, watched them with angry eyes.

'What a funny family you've got,' Michael remarked to her, trying to make conversation.

Her head went up with a jerk.

'Funny? What do you mean funny, pray – funny?'

'Well – odd. Mr Turvy turning Catherine wheels and standing on his head—'

Mary Poppins stared at him as though she could not believe her ears.

'Did I understand you to say,' she began, speaking her words as though she were biting them, 'that my cousin turned a Catherine wheel? And stood on—'

'But he did,' protested Michael nervously. 'We saw him.'

'On his head? A relation of mine on his head? And turning about like a firework display?' Mary Poppins seemed hardly able to repeat the dreadful statement. She glared at Michael.

'Now this,' she began, and he shrank back in terror from her wild darting eyes, 'this is the Last Straw. First you are impudent to me and then you insult my relations. It would take very little more – Very Little More – to make me give notice. So – I warn you!'

And with that she bounced round on her seat and sat with her back to them. And even from the back she looked angrier than they had ever seen her.

Michael leant forward.

'I—I apologise,' he said.

There was no answer from the seat in front.

'I'm sorry, Mary Poppins!'

'Humph!'

'*Very* sorry!'

'And well you might be!' she retorted, staring straight ahead of her.

Michael leant towards Jane.

'But it was true – what I said. Wasn't it?' he whispered.

Jane shook her head and put her finger to her lip. She was staring at Mary Poppins' hat. And presently, when she was sure that Mary Poppins was not looking, she pointed to the brim.

There, gleaming on the black shiny straw, was a scattering of crumbs, yellow crumbs from a sponge cake, the kind of thing you would expect to find on the hat of a person who had stood on their head to have Tea.

Michael gazed at the crumbs for a moment. Then he turned and nodded understandingly to Jane.

They sat there, jogging up and down as the bus rumbled homewards. Mary Poppins' back, erect and angry, was like a silent warning. They dared not speak to her. But every time the bus turned a corner they saw the crumbs turning Catherine wheels on the shining brim of her hat . . .

Secrets

Anita Desai
Illustrated by Rachael Saunders

One morning, at school, Rohan got every single sum wrong. Then he dropped a bottle of ink on the floor and it splashed on to his teacher's white canvas shoes. When he made a face behind his teacher's back, he was seen. So he had to be punished.

'Here, take this letter to your father and go home,' his teacher said, after writing a long and angry letter. 'Let him punish you as well.'

Rohan tried to look too proud to care, and picked up his books and walked out of the school yard and up the narrow city lane. But once he reached the big grey banyan tree that was the only tree in the lane, and found that the cobbler who usually sat under it, mending broken old shoes, was not there, he sat down in its shade, hiding himself in the folds of the great trunk, and sobbed a little with anger. He had not been able to get his sums right although he had tried. He had dropped the ink bottle by accident and not to spoil the teacher's white shoes. Perhaps it was bad of him to pull a face but how could he help it when things were going so badly? Now he was afraid to go home and hand the letter to his father, who might be a little cross.

So Rohan hid there in the folds of the grey tree trunk, and poked with a stick at the seeds dropped on the ground by the parrots that ate the red berries of the tree. He was so angry and afraid that he poked and poked with the stick till he had dug quite a deep hole in the dust. In that hole he found a little grey lump of rubber – a plain piece of rubber that some other schoolboy might have dropped there long ago. He picked it up and rolled it about between his fingers.

'I wish it were a magic rubber,' he said, sobbing a little. 'I would rub out the whole school, like this – like this—' and he stepped out to look down the lane at the boys' school that stood at the end of it, and angrily rubbed at the air with the grey lump of rubber.

Then he stopped, his hand still in mid-air, his mouth still open, and his hair began to stand up on his head as it did on his neighbour's cat's back when she saw his dog.

Something very, very strange had happened. The school had vanished. He had really rubbed it out! The tall, three-storey house on its left, with its latticed balconies and green roof, was still there, and on the other side the tin-roofed warehouse where timber was stacked stood there, too, but in between them, where the school had been, there was now a patch of earth. There was no white school building, no deep verandas, no dusty playground, no high grey wall and not a single schoolboy. There was just a square of bare brown earth between the other buildings, all quiet and still now in the heat of the afternoon.

Rohan's knees were shaking. He ran a little way down the road to see better but still could find nothing but a blank where the school had once been. Then he felt so afraid of the vanished school that he ran back up the lane as fast as he could, snatched up his books and the terrible rubber from among the roots of the banyan, and ran into the road where he lived. He hurried up the stairs at the side of the little yellow house to their room on the roof where his mother hung the clothes to dry and his father stacked old boxes and bicycle tyres.

His mother was alone at home. She was

kneading dough in a big brass pan. The fire was not yet lit. 'You're early,' she said, in surprise. 'I haven't any food ready for you yet. But you can go and break up an old box and get me some wood to light the fire. I'll warm some milk for you. Hurry up, don't look so sulky,' she said, and began to roll and thump the dough in the pan, roll and thump, roll and thump, so she did not see the face Rohan made as he went out to pull an old crate to pieces and bring in an armload of packing-case wood.

He came in and threw it all into the grate with such force that the ashes and grit flew up and settled on all the pots and pans, and the dough and the neat floor as well.

His mother was so angry, she shouted, 'What's the matter with you, you rascal? Look what you've done! What a mess you've made! Now go and fetch the broom and sweep it up at once.'

'I won't sweep,' he shouted back, as loudly as though there were a devil in him, shouting for him.

She was still more angry. 'I won't sweep it up either. Let it lie there and then your father will see it when he comes home,' she said.

Then Rohan felt so afraid that he held up the magic rubber and cried, 'I won't let you do that. I won't let him see it. I'll – I'll rub you all out,' and he swept through the air with the little grey lump of rubber, as hard as he could. He shut his eyes tight because his face was all screwed up with anger, and when he opened them the whole house with the unlit fire, the brass pan, the glass of milk and even his mother had vanished. There was only the roof-top, blazing in the afternoon sun, littered with empty tins and old tyres at the edges but quite, quite bare in the middle.

Now Rohan did not have a home or a mother or even a glass of milk. His mouth hung open, he was so frightened by what he had done. Then he turned and ran down the stairs as fast as he could, so that his father would not come and find him standing alone on the empty roof-top.

He heard an excited bark and saw it was his dog, Kalo, who had been sleeping in the shade of an overturned basket in a corner of the roof-top, but had heard him run down the stairs and followed him. Kalo was frightened, too, at the way their room had disappeared and the roof-top left standing empty, so he was running along behind Rohan, barking with fright.

Rohan felt afraid that the people who lived in the yellow house would come out and see what had happened, so he shouted 'Go back, Kalo! Go back!' But Kalo ran towards him, his long black ears flapping as he ran. So Rohan rubbed the air with his rubber again and screamed, 'I don't want you! Go away!' and Kalo vanished. His round paw marks were still to be seen in the dust of the road. A little trail of dust was still hanging in the hot, still air of that dreadful afternoon, but Kalo the dog had vanished.

And someone had seen. An old man who traded in empty tins and bottles had just started his evening round and, while shouting 'Tin and bo—' stopped short and stared till Rohan, rubbing in the air with his rubber again, shouted, 'You can't see! You mustn't see!' and rubbed him out. That old man with his grey beard and big sack of clanking tins and bottles just disappeared as Kalo had.

Then Rohan turned and ran even faster. He ran into the big road that went round the mosque. Just in time he remembered that he might meet his father there, for he had a cycle repair shop at the foot of the mosque steps. So he whirled around again. He kept going in circles, as if he were a little mad. At last he ran to the banyan tree, climbed over its roots into a cleft between two folds of the huge trunk and hid there, trembling.

'I'll hide this terrible rubber,' he said at

last. 'I'll put it back in the hole and never, never take it out again.' With shaking fingers he scraped more dust from the little hole he had dug earlier, in order to bury the rubber.

As he scraped and dug with trembling fingers, he found something else in the hole. At first he saw only one end of it – it was long and yellow. He dug harder and found it was a pencil. Quite a new pencil – he could see no one had used it before, though it looked old from being buried in the earth. He stopped crying and trembling as he wondered who could have buried a pencil here, and whether it was a magic pencil as the rubber was a magic one. He had to try it and see.

First he dropped the rubber into the hole and covered it up. Then he held up the pencil and pointed it at the bare patch of earth where the school had once stood between the warehouse and the green-roofed house. Very, very carefully he drew a picture of his old white school building in the air. He did it so carefully that he seemed to see the grey lines forming before his eyes. Then he blinked: the grey-white building really *was* there now. Or was it only a picture in his mind? Quickly he drew the verandas, the playground, the high wall, and then the little matchstick figures of a line of schoolboys rushing out of the front gate, the lane filling with them, and saw them leaping and running with their satchels flying behind them.

He stood up and ran a little way down the lane, out of the shade of the mysteriously whispering banyan tree. Now, in the clear sunlight, he could see the school quite plainly again, alive and noisy with children set free from their lessons. He stood there till he saw the teacher come out on his bicycle. Then he turned and ran the other way up the lane.

He stood in the middle of the dusty road and quickly, quickly, drew a picture of a little black dog in the air, as well as he could. He was still working on the long plumed tail when he heard Kalo bark, and saw him bounce down on to the road on his four feet and come pelting towards him.

As he came closer, Rohan saw he had missed out the jagged edge of Kalo's ear where it had been torn in a dogfight. He was careful to add that so Kalo would be exactly as he had been before, scarred and dusty and wild with happiness. Kalo stood still, waiting for him to finish.

When it was done, he shouted 'Kalo! Kalo!' and patted him hastily, then went on busily with his pencil, drawing the old, bearded tin-and-bottle man. He was just drawing the big, bulging sack when he heard the cracked voice cry '-o-ttle man!' and there he was, shuffling down the road and blinking a little in the bright light.

Then Rohan and his dog ran home, up the stairs to the empty rooftop. There, leaning against the low wall, his tongue between his teeth and his eyes narrowed, Rohan drew a picture of his home as well as he could. Even when he could see it quite plainly, the little whitewashed room with its arched windows and pigeon-roost on the flat roof, he went on

drawing. He drew a picture of his mother kneading dough in a pan, the fire, the glass of milk and even the broom in the corner of the room. Then he went in and found them all there, just as he had drawn them. But he saw one mistake he had made in his drawing – he had coloured his mother's hair black and left out the grey strands over her ears. She had remained stiff, lifeless. He stood in the doorway, rubbing gently at the unnatural darkness of her hair till it showed the grey he knew. He realised you cannot draw a picture out of desperation, or with careless speed. It took care, attention, time.

When he had finished, his mother moved, looked up at him. 'There's your milk,' she said quietly, 'drink it up.'

He nodded. 'I'll sweep up a bit first,' he

said, and went to fetch the broom. He swept and he swept, enjoying the work that he had not wanted to do at first, till he heard his father arrive, lean his bicycle against the wall and lock it, then come slowly up the stairs.

Rohan ran out, shouting 'Look, I found a pencil and a rubber on the road today.' He wanted so much to tell his father all about it and ask him how it happened, but he did not dare.

His father was looking tired. 'Why don't you sit quietly and draw something?' he said, as he went in for his tea.

Rohan nodded and went to fetch a piece of paper. Then he sat on the top step and spread out the paper and drew. He was not sure if the magic pencil would draw an ordinary picture. It did. Using it very, very carefully now, he drew a picture of Kalo.

When his father saw it, he beamed. He had never seen a picture as good. Rohan showed it to his mother too, and she was so pleased she pinned it on the wall, next to the calendar.

His father said, 'I didn't know you could draw so well. Your teacher never told us. You should draw a picture for him.'

Rohan spent the whole evening drawing with the magic pencil. He took the drawings to school next day, and his teacher was so pleased with them that he forgot to ask for an answer to his angry letter of the day before. He gave Rohan good paper and time to draw every day.

Rohan drew so much that the magic pencil

was soon worn to a stub. Instead of throwing it away like an ordinary pencil, he took it down to the banyan tree and buried it in the earth at its roots where he had hidden the lump of rubber. As he walked away he worried about whether he would be able to draw as well with an ordinary pencil bought at the stationery shop near the school gate. But he had had so much practice now, and become so good an artist, that he found he could do as good a drawing with the new pencil he bought as with the magic one.

He became so famous in that town that people came from miles away to see the pictures his mother pinned to the walls of their house. They went to the school and asked the teacher about him. No one knew how he had learnt to draw and paint so well without any lessons or help. Even when he became a great artist, whose name was known all over the land, Rohan did not tell anyone the story. That was his secret – and the banyan tree's.

The Old Stone Faces

Ann Pilling
Illustrated by Ruthine Burton

Every day, on his way to school, Joe Parker walked with his mother past the old stone faces.

The Parkers lived in a small flat over the tuck-shop in Holywell Street, where Joe's mum was kept busy all day, selling newspapers and sweets and tobacco to all the people who walked up and down that dark, twisty street, one of the oldest and most mysterious in the whole of Oxford. It is a city full of the most fascinating and curious things, but nothing fascinated Joe Parker more than the old stone faces stuck up above some railings round an ancient yellowy-stone building in Broad Street.

There were seventeen of them, all in a row, and each one was different. Seventeen massive stone heads, with stone hair and stone beards, staring out across the traffic at the students going in and out of Blackwell's bookshop. Some of the faces were sad and bored-looking, others were grumpy. Joe's favourite was old Goggle-Eyes who looked as if he'd just seen a ghost. But though they were all different,

the seventeen faces had one thing in common – they all looked extremely miserable, and Joe felt sorry for them.

'Come on, Joe,' his mum said one day when they were rushing to school as usual. 'Staring at those funny old statues again! Do hurry up, or we'll be late.'

'Who put them there, Mum?' Joe asked as they went along. 'What are they for? And why do they look so fed up?'

Mrs Parker wasn't really listening. Her head was full of the things she had to do when she got back to the sweetshop. There was the new paper boy to talk to, and the ice-cream people to phone, and the old professor's special tobacco to order from the suppliers.

'There must be *somebody* who could tell

me about them, Mum,' Joe was saying. 'Surely *somebody* must know.'

It was his mother's turn to stop in the middle of the street. She'd had an idea.

'There is, Joe. I've just thought of the very person. Why don't you ask Professor Owen Morgan Jones? He's sure to know. They say he's the oldest professor in Oxford. He'll be in to collect his special tobacco on Friday. You could ask him then.'

'I *will*' said Joe.

But when Friday came, the rain was pouring down, and Holywell Street was as black as night.

'Joe,' Mrs Parker said. 'Put your anorak on, will you, and pop down to number thirty with Professor Jones's tobacco.'

Two minutes later Joe was knocking on the professor's door.

'Come in, Joe,' said a whispery old Welsh voice. 'Come in and get warm, it's a nasty old day.'

Soon Joe was sitting by a roaring fire with a mug of hot cocoa and some ginger biscuits.

'My mum sent you the special tobacco,' he said. 'And . . . and . . .' Then he stopped. He felt rather frightened of Professor Owen Morgan Jones. There was something mysterious about him. His small sharp eyes were such a bright green, and his beard was the whitest and bushiest Joe had ever seen. He looked centuries old.

'You've got something to ask me, haven't

you?' the professor said, opening the tobacco and filling his pipe.

'How do you know?' Joe asked in surprise.

The old man laughed. 'You don't live as long as I have, Joe, if you don't keep your wits about you, and your ears open. I'm the oldest professor in Oxford, you know. Well, what's your question?'

'It's about those statues in Broad Street, the big stone heads on top of the railings. What are they there for? And why do they look so unhappy?'

Professor Owen Morgan Jones puffed on his pipe.

'People have argued about those heads for years and years, Joe, and none of them knows the true story. Some say they're great Roman emperors, or old Greek poets. Others say they might be advertisements for various kinds of beard – you'll have noticed that all their beards are different, I suppose?'

'I have,' Joe said. 'But that doesn't explain why they all look so miserable.'

Suddenly the professor clutched at his sleeve in excitement. '*That*,' he cried, 'is the most important question of all! Clever boy to have asked such a question! The fact is, Joe, that those stone heads are not kings or poets or advertisements at all. Those are the heads of nothing less than the *Pontybodkin Male Voice Choir*.'

'The *what*?' Joe said.

'The Pontybodkin Male Voice Choir!' Professor Jones repeated. 'One of the most wonderful choirs in Wales. Many years ago they came here and gave a special concert at the Town Hall. It was a marvellous concert, Joe, the whole of Oxford came to listen to them, the tickets were sold out months ahead. But when it was over, and they were going back to Pontybodkin, something terrible happened.'

'What?' Joe whispered.

'A spell was cast upon them, by the Witches of Wellington Square.'

When he heard this Joe nearly jumped out of his skin. 'Are there really witches in Wellington Square?' he stammered. 'That's the way I go to school. We walk through there every day, me and my mum.'

Professor Jones took his hand and squeezed it.

'It's all right, Joe, they left Oxford years ago.'

'Why?'

'Well, nobody liked them very much, and *they* didn't like the climate. They complained that it was too foggy and damp. So they emigrated. But the night of the concert – you do know that witches can't sing, I suppose?'

'No, I didn't,' Joe said.

'Well, they can't. Anyway, on the night of the concert they sat outside the Town Hall, blocking the pavement with their broomsticks, howling jealously in chorus while the glorious singing was going on inside. Nobody listened to them, of course, and a policeman moved them on in the end. But what do you think they did?'

Joe shook his head.

'They glided off down the Banbury Road and hid themselves in some big trees, waiting for the Pontybodkin Male Voice Choir to drive past on its way home. It was a cold rainy night, very like this one, and the coach driver didn't look back till he was well on the road to Wales. But after a few miles he turned round and said, "Well, lads, it was a right royal performance tonight. How about a few songs for me?" And do you know what, Joe? That coach was completely empty and all that was left of the Pontybodkin Male Voice Choir was a row of stone heads in Broad Street.'

There was silence in the small, dark room, and Joe listened to the rain clattering against the window. Professor Owen Morgan Jones stared into the fire sadly.

'Such singing, Joe. So beautiful. It would almost break your heart. I should like to hear it just once more, before I die. Will you help me?'

Without waiting for Joe's answer the old man had climbed on to a stool and was lifting an enormous book down from a shelf. He spread it open on his knees and began to look through it. At last he stopped, and read down a page carefully.

'Here it is, Joe. Here we have it. This tells us how to—'

'To bring back the Pontybodkin Male Voice Choir?' Joe interrupted in excitement.

'Not quite, Joe. You see, they've been up on those railings a bit too long really, and when the Witches of Wellington Square emigrated they crossed the sea – and that always strengthens their kind of magic. But at least this book tells us how to make the heads sing again. I'll need your help though.'

'But, Professor Jones,' Joe said, 'why don't you make them sing yourself?'

'I'm too old, Joe,' he said wistfully. 'The book says that what must be done can only be done by a small boy, someone about your age. How old are you?'

'Seven and a half,' Joe said nervously.

'That's perfect then. Will you do it?'

'Well, I'll have a go,' said Joe.

A few minutes later it was all arranged. Professor Jones copied something down from the old book, folded the piece of paper, and pushed it into Joe's hand.

'Take it home, Joe, keep it safe. Don't read it yet, but when the time comes, take it with you.'

'But how will I know *when* the time has come?' Joe asked, feeling rather bewildered.

'To release the Pontybodkin Male Voice Choir,' Professor Jones said triumphantly, 'three things are required: a clear moonlit night, a pure black cat, and the words you've just put into your pocket. A moonlit night's no problem, though we may have to wait a bit. You've not got a pure black cat, I suppose?'

'I'm afraid not,' Joe said.

'Don't worry. One'll turn up eventually, it always does. Now off you go. Your mother'll be wondering what's happened to you.'

The squally weather lasted for ages. Joe didn't bother to check on the clear moonlit night because he knew there must be thick clouds all over the sky, and in any case the pure black cat hadn't shown up yet.

There were hundreds of cats in Oxford, tabby and tawny, marmalade and grey, black cats with white paws, white cats with black paws, cats that slipped out from alleyways and rubbed against his legs, cats that peered down at him from crumbling old walls. Once, in the pet shop, Joe thought they'd found the cat they needed, but when it was lifted out of the window he spotted three white hairs under its chin, and he turned away in disappointment.

'I'm sorry,' he said to the lady. 'But you see, it has to be pure black.'

Then, one night, when he was asleep, bright moonlight shone into his eyes and woke him up. He got out of bed and tiptoed across to the window to look out. The night was thick with stars, and the most brilliant moon Joe had ever seen was floating across the sky. *It was time.*

Quickly he felt under his mattress for Professor Jones's piece of paper. Then he crept downstairs, through the shop, and stepped outside into the cold crisp night.

Seconds later he was standing in Broad Street in front of the railings, staring up at the big carved faces. The dead stone eyes stared back at him coldly, and the stone beards twinkled with frost.

Joe looked down and saw a tiny black cat sitting on the pavement, its face raised to his expectantly. Its tail was curved like a question mark as if to say, 'I'm ready, Joe. Are you?'

'What do we do first, I wonder?' Joe said aloud, and at once the little cat took a flying leap upwards and landed neatly on the great stone head at the end of the row.

It stayed there for a minute, peeping down through the carved stone curls, dabbing at the long stone nose with its paws, then it leaped on to the next head, and the next, until every one of those seventeen statues had felt the warm, soft paws of the furry little cat on its icy-cold face.

As the cat leapt from head to head something amazing happened. The faces came to life. One wrinkled its nose and sneezed loudly, another yawned and cleared its throat, a third shook its head violently and opened and shut its mouth several times. Then they all peered round at each other curiously and when they saw their friends were awake too their big stone faces were wreathed in smiles.

But none of them spoke. They were all nodding and winking at each other silently, and looking up at the stars, as if to say, 'It's a fine night, mates!'

Suddenly, Joe remembered the piece of paper. He unfolded it carefully and read it through under a street lamp, then he spoke the simple words aloud, in a firm clear voice:

'Stone men of Wales,
Silent so long,
Awake! And thrill this city
With your song!'

And as the last words of the spell echoed along Broad Street the seventeen men of the Pontybodkin Male Voice Choir opened their mouths, and sang.

Miraculous singing it was, as rich and as mellow as ripe fruit. The great sound rose up and floated out over the frosty rooftops as Joe stood by the railings with the black cat purring in his arms, his whole body tingling as he listened to the most wonderful music he had ever heard.

They warmed up with a few short songs in Welsh, and with 'Land of My Fathers and Men of Harlech'. Then, after a pause for a bit of coughing and clearing of throats, they burst into a great hymn:

'Guide me, O thou great Jehovah,
Pilgrim through this barren land!'

All along Holywell Street doors were opening, sash windows were being pushed up, heads were popping out. From Catte Street and Ship Street, from George Street and St Giles', people were coming to hear the strange singing, for the miracle of the music had woven itself into their dreams.

In no time at all Broad Street was filled with people in pyjamas, yawning students and landladies in flowery dressing gowns, all bleary-eyed and happy as they listened, and the Pontybodkin Male Voice Choir sang on and on, making up for all its years of silence with marvellous song, as the clocks of the city crept steadily on towards midnight.

'They'll do *requests*!' the crowds whispered to each other in excitement. 'Let's see if they'll sing something for us. Let's ask for the old favourites. Go on, you ask them . . . no, *you* ask them . . .'

And they sang a Latin school-song for two rumple-headed students in yellow pyjamas:

'Gaudeamus igitur Iuvenes dum sumus!'

they bellowed joyfully. And they sang 'Pack Up Your Troubles in Your Old Kit-Bag' for the park keeper who'd once been a soldier. And for Mrs Mutton, the old widow-lady who lived next door to Joe, they sang a quiet verse of 'God Be with You Till We Meet Again', and when they sang this the tears rolled down their stone cheeks, and splashed on to the pavement.

Suddenly, high up on a tower, a church clock rang out. It was a quarter to twelve. The choir finished Mrs Mutton's request and fell silent. A shiver went through the crowd and people muttered 'Don't pack it up yet, lads. Give us another song!' And the cry was taken up on all sides. 'More! More! We want more!'

'Silence, all of you!' a stern Welsh voice shouted from somewhere at the back. 'There is one more song to come. Silence, and you will hear.' And then the Pontybodkin Male Voice Choir broke into the mightiest song of all:

'Hallelujah! Hallelujah!
For the Lord God Omnipotent reigneth!'

The little black cat had jumped out of Joe's arms and was lost in the crowd. He felt cold suddenly, but then a warm hand was slipped into his. It was the professor.

'Thank you, Joe,' he said. 'You did it. I knew you would.'

'And He shall reign for ever and ever! Hallelujah!'

the choir sang out. Professor Owen Morgan Jones stood there listening, with the little boy at his side. And the glory of it filled the city.

Joe felt terribly sleepy next day as he hurried along Broad Street, at the last minute as usual. His mum didn't know what a late night they'd had, he and the professor. She slept

118

at the back of their flat, and she hadn't heard a thing.

When he looked across the road at the heads Joe half-expected them to have disappeared. But they were there all right, all seventeen of them, and he did think they looked just a little less miserable than usual.

Fishing with Dicky

Sally Christie
Illustrated by Rachael Saunders

L ast summer, my brother, Dicky, got a
fishing rod. He fished all through the
holidays and I fished with him. I fished with
my net, though sometimes Dicky let me hold
the rod. I caught tiddlers in the shallows;

Dicky caught dace and roach and – once – a trout.

When the holidays were over, Dicky went to his new school.

I'm still at Tidshore Primary. I'm younger than Dicky, see.

'More peas?' said Mum.

I shook my head and covered my plate with my hands. I love frozen peas when they're frozen but they're boring when they're cooked.

'Manners,' said Mum. '*No, thank you.* Dicky?'

'No, thanks,' he said.

'It'll have to be you then, Phil. All right?'

'I won't say no,' said Dad, making room on his plate.

Mum got up and went to the cooker. 'Two fish fingers left,' she announced. 'Any takers?'

'Me!' I shouted.

'Pre-packed, over-priced rubbish,' said Dad.

'I've got to go,' said Dicky.

It was always like that when we had fish fingers now. Sooner or later Dad would make a pointed remark and Dicky would leave. You see, Dad had loved it over the summer, when Dicky had brought home fish from the river, and he couldn't get used to things having changed. When Dicky and I had come home with the trout, and Mum had cooked it with butter and almonds, Dad had opened a bottle of wine. He and Mum had clinked glasses and Dad had said, 'Here's to our fisherman! Long may he fish! Who needs fish fingers when we've got Dicky!'

'Give over, Dad,' Dicky had said, but he'd smiled.

To me, the best thing about that trout had been the almonds. I never liked eating the fish Dicky caught. I felt sorry for their poor, cooked heads and their dried-up eyes; I choked on their bones; and – when Mum told me to stop holding my nose – all I could taste was river.

Give me fish fingers any day! I thought as Mum delivered one of the two from the cooker to my plate. But I missed not going fishing with Dicky any more. It wasn't as if *he'd* stopped going: just that things had changed.

Dicky was already up, shoving his chair under the table, taking his plate to the sink.

'Fishing?' said Dad, as if he didn't know.

'Yep,' said Dicky.

'Good luck!' said Dad, as if he really thought there was some point in saying it.

Dicky slammed the door and was gone.

'Oh dear,' sighed Mum. 'I wish you wouldn't go upsetting him like that, Phil.'

'*Me* upsetting *him!*' said Dad. 'What about the other way round? If he's so sensitive about fish fingers, why doesn't he bring us some of the real thing? I don't know what's come over him, I really don't. There's something going on.'

I folded up the crispy, golden coating of my last fish finger, which I'd carefully peeled off and saved, and popped it into my mouth with a big 'Ahhh!' Mum looked at me and winked.

'*We* know why Dicky's not catching anything these days, don't we?' she said. 'He's not taking his lucky charm – his lucky Charlie – that's why not!' (No, I'm not a boy, in case you're wondering. Charlie's short for Charlotte.)

'And that's another thing,' said Dad.

'Now, Phil,' said Mum. 'We've been through all this before. New school – new friends. It's nice for him to be in with a group. Of course they don't want little sisters around. And how much fish they catch is their business.'

Dad just grunted.

'What's for afters?' I said.

I'm not like Dad. If I were, I'd have asked, 'Can I come?' every time Dicky picked up his rod. But I knew what the answer would have been, so I didn't. I didn't think I'd be fishing with Dicky ever again. But there I was wrong.

Two days after the day of that fish finger tea, Dad's aged aunt died. The funeral was to be on Saturday, and Mum and Dad were both going. They'd be away the whole day, because Great-Aunt Anne had lived a long way off: it would take them hours and hours to get there, and hours and hours to get back.

'So, Dicky,' said Mum, 'you'll have to look after Charlie. Gran can't come over because she's going to the funeral too, and Charlie can't go next door because next door are away.'

'Can't I go round to Susan's?' I said quickly. I didn't want to hear Dicky saying he didn't want me.

'Sorry,' said Mum. 'I spoke to Susan's mum at the school gates this morning: Susan's with her dad this weekend.'

I shot a glance at Dicky. He looked furious. Then:

'Why me?' he burst out.

'I've just told you, silly,' said Mum. 'There's no one else. Anyway, you can have a good time together. I'll give you money for the pictures, if you like.'

'Yeah!' I said. 'Let's go to the pictures, Dicky!' Everything was going to be all right, after all. But:

'I'm going fishing,' said Dicky.

'Then you take Charlie with you,' said Mum. She was getting impatient. Dad was washing up, and I knew she wanted to get back to the kitchen to check he wasn't using the scratchy wire thing on the plates.

'She'll fall in the river,' said Dicky.

'I won't!' I said.

'Oh, for goodness' sake, Dicky, *of course* she won't,' said Mum. 'How many times have you fished together before? And how many times has Charlie fallen in? So don't give me *that*. If you've a *real* reason – and I don't expect to be told what it is – then you can just give fishing a miss for once. Go to the pictures instead. All I'm saying is, wherever you go, Charlie goes too.'

'I'm going fishing,' said Dicky.

'Fine,' said Mum, and dived into the kitchen.

'Oh gawd,' said Dicky.

'I don't want to go stupid fishing, anyway,' I said.

'Oh *gawd*,' said Dicky.

I'd meant it when I'd said that I didn't want to go fishing, but as Saturday came closer I got more and more excited. I couldn't help it: I remembered those days in the summer when

Dicky and I had sat on the river bank side by side, Dicky's float bobbing mid-stream, my net lurking in the water just beyond our toes. A minnow would dart in; I wouldn't dare move. 'Dicky,' I'd whisper. 'Look.' Dicky doesn't move either, but he sees.

'Steady, Charlie, bring it up slowly.'

My hands tighten on the handle of the net and I start easing it upwards, pushing against the current, wondering when the minnow will realise what's going on. The minnow darts again, but not quite out. 'Steady, steady,' breathes Dicky. And then my net breaks the surface of the water and I yell and there's a tiny sliver of silver flipping around inside, on the green plastic mesh.

Before I learnt to listen to Dicky, I always yanked the net up as soon as I saw a fish swim

in. And the fish was always quicker than me. 'They always will be,' said Dicky. 'You have to get them with skill, not speed.'

Skill, not speed – skill, not speed I chanted to myself, going to bed on Friday night. And I didn't count sheep when I couldn't get to sleep: I counted little, darting fishes – into my net.

Next morning, Mum and Dad left early. Mum had made two boxes of sandwiches for Dicky and me to take with us for lunch: they were there on the table when I came into the kitchen with my net. Dicky was in there too, fiddling about with his open-face fixed-spool reel. It looked like the body of a tiny, shiny motorbike, and Dicky was always doing things to it, like a motorbike mechanic making adjustments to his machine.

I picked up one of the sandwich boxes.

'I'm ready,' I said.

Dicky glanced up. 'You're not having that.'

'Oh, sorry,' I said. 'Didn't know they were different.' I put the box back on the table and picked up the other one. Maybe Mum had made Dicky egg mayonnaise, which were his favourite. Maybe mine were peanut butter and banana.

Dicky glanced up again. 'No, *that*.' He meant my net.

'But we're going fishing,' I said, 'aren't we?'

'*I'm* going fishing.'

'But Mum said . . .'

'*I'm* going fishing, you're tagging along. You're coming with me but you're not going to fish.'

We had a really big argument then. Dicky

said his friends wouldn't want someone poking about in the water with a kiddy's seaside toy. This was serious fishing, he said. I said, if it was so serious, how come he never caught any fish? I reckoned he didn't want me to take my net because he was afraid I'd catch a tiddler – and that would be more than he'd done in the last three weeks!

We went on and on, round and round, until Dicky suddenly looked at his watch. 'Now I'm going to be late,' he said. 'You coming or not?'

As I stomped past him through the back door, he snatched the net from my hand. I made a horrible face but said nothing.

That September was very mild. It was like summer slowly fading, not winter coming on.

Cycling along behind Dicky – cycling as fast as I could, to keep up – the wind rushed fresh but not cold in my face. It blew away my rage about the net. I began to feel excited again.

'Dicky!' I shouted. 'Slow down!'

It didn't really matter that he was drawing further and further ahead because I knew the way to the river perfectly. But I wanted to let him know that I was speaking to him again.

'Dick-y!'

I thought he was going to ignore me, till I heard him jam on his brakes. And then he didn't just slow down: he stopped. I came up beside him, puffing and laughing.

'Dicky, I—'

'Another thing you've got to get into your head,' he said. 'From now on, I'm not Dicky. I'm Rich.'

Still I puffed, but I stopped laughing. I was puzzled. I stared into Dicky's face.

'*Rich*,' he said. 'Okay?'

'But Dicky's your name and . . .'

'Richard's my real name. And now I want you to call me Rich.'

'But you're not Rich, you're Dicky!'

'I'm *Rich*!' he shouted, and thudded my handlebar with his fist. 'Dicky's a stupid name. I'll chuck you in the river if you call me it today. Rich, Rich, Rich! It's important.'

He got back on his bike and set off again. I followed. I was a little scared now. Not scared of Dicky, but scared because now I knew he was.

He was out of sight by the time I turned off the road down the Petherton bridleway, but when I reached the farm track that led to the river, he was waiting for me. The track was too rough to ride along, so we got off our bikes and pushed them. We'd always done that, but in the old days we used to talk as we went.

There were two boys on the bank when we arrived. Two boys, two bikes, two boxes of sandwiches. The boys looked about Dicky's age, though one was quite a lot bigger than him.

Two boys, two bikes, two sandwich boxes. But only one rod. The smaller of the boys wasn't fishing but just sitting, stirring their tinful of maggots with his finger.

'Wotcha,' said Dicky.

'You're late,' said Big Boy.

'Hey, Rich, that a new kind of maggot you've got?' said Maggot Boy.

'Sorry, Max,' said Dicky, looking at Big Boy. 'She's my sister. Got to look after her today. Couldn't get out of it.'

'When you come in with us,' said Max, 'that doesn't mean you get a family pass.' He swore. 'You'll be bringing your granny along tomorrow!'

Maggot Boy laughed as if that were the best thing he'd heard all year.

'Shut yer gob!' said Max, and to Dicky: 'Oh, forget it. Tell her to play with her dolls or something – over by the fence.'

The fence he meant was a line of posts and rails separating the river bank from a great grassy field. There were cows in the field, distant blobs of black and white.

'Get over by the fence,' muttered Dicky, and I went.

I like cows, actually. I like their big dark eyes and the way they'll wrap their tongues round a tussock of grass and tug. I liked the idea of the cows in that field much more than I liked Dicky's friends. So I turned my back on the river and began picking grass to offer to the cows.

It was quite a while before I'd got a bunch that I thought would be enough to attract their attention. When I had, I climbed on to the fence and waved it above my head.

'MOOOOO!' I shouted.

The cows took no notice, but someone behind me swore.

'Tell her to shut her gob,' came Max's voice.

'Shut up, Charlotte,' said Dicky.

I was so surprised to hear him call me that – no one ever calls me that – that I swivelled round on the fence. And what I *saw* surprised me even more. I let my bunch of grass fall to the ground. Now I knew why Dicky didn't catch anything these days. The answer was simple – though I couldn't understand it.

Dicky didn't fish.

Max fished and now Maggot Boy fished – using Max's rod. (It had what looked like an old kite reel tied on to the handle with a shoe-lace.) Dicky's rod – the rod that Uncle Ed had given him for his birthday – Dicky's rod with its beautiful, shiny, open-face fixed-spool reel – was in Max's fat red hands.

Dicky sat by Max, watching Max's float. Nobody spoke.

And then Max's float twitched. Straight off, Dicky said, 'Steady, steady.' I wondered how long it had taken Max to learn to listen to Dicky's advice.

Well, Dicky talked Max through the catch, and Max, like a robot, did what Dicky said, and soon there was a biggish fish – a roach, I think – dangling over the water, on the end of Max's line.

'*YES!*' yelled Max, as if he were punching the air with the word.

'Max-a-*million!*' said Maggot Boy.

Dicky just reached out and quietly unhooked the roach.

The fish he used to catch in the old days he'd knocked on the head at once. He said it was painless to kill them that way, and the sooner you did it, the kinder it was. I'd always thrown back my minnows, except once when I'd sneaked one home in a jam jar – and Dicky had been furious then. 'You're cruel,' he'd said. 'A fish like that needs running water.' And sure enough, by the time we'd set out for the river again, the minnow was dead.

But here was Max telling Dicky not to kill the roach, and here was Dicky emptying sandwiches from one of our boxes and filling the box with water and slipping the live roach in.

'I'll see to him when we're done,' said Max. Then Maggot Boy passed him a maggot and he hooked it and cast his line again.

I couldn't understand it. I crept forward to look at the roach in the box. It lay straight and still, like a silver spearhead. Its nose was pressed into one corner, its tail splayed out against another. Some crumbs from our sandwiches floated above its head.

I felt more sorry for this fish, with its sleek reddish fins and pumping gills, than I'd ever felt for the fish Mum cooked till their fins were charred and their eyes dull and crinkly. 'Poor thing,' I whispered, and reached out to stroke it.

I don't know whether I'd even touched it, when the body suddenly flexed and thrashed.

SSHLOCK! The sides of the sandwich box jolted, and for an instant the water churned. Then, while water still splattered on the ground round about, the fish was a silver spearhead again.

I was so surprised, I just crouched there and stared.

'Oi!' said Max, half-turning. 'Get her away from that!'

Dicky shuffled round on his bottom and ordered me back to the fence.

'And she'd better stay there,' said Maggot Boy. 'Tormenting helpless creatures. It's cruel.'

Back by the fence, I stuck out my tongue at him, but he was prodding maggots in the tin, and didn't see. I think he preferred prodding maggots to fishing.

The cows had moved closer, but only by chance, it seemed. I sat down on the ground with my back against a fence post. In front of me, the boys sat in a line on the bank; halfway between us sat the box with the fish in it.

I felt cross with myself for having tried to

stroke the roach. How stupid that had been! Just because the roach was there, imprisoned in the sandwich box, I'd thought that that had made it suddenly tame. Stupid, stupid, stupid. I'd thought . . . But then I realised that I hadn't thought at all.

I was feeling crosser and crosser, wanting to kick myself or pull my own hair – when something really weird happened. Somebody else pulled it for me, from behind. Not just pulled, either: tugged, dragged and went on dragging.

'*DICKY*!' I screeched, as I was hauled to my feet.

Heading backwards through the fence, I twisted round and saw – a cow!

For a moment I looked into her big dark eyes; knew (though couldn't see) that she'd

144

wrapped her tongue round my ponytail. And then Dicky was there, clapping his hands and shouting, 'SHOOO!' And the cow let go.

My scalp felt as though I'd been dragged twice round the world, though actually I hadn't even gone right through to the field. I clutched my head.

'You all right?' said Dicky.

I nodded. I saw that in the field *all* the cows had gathered to stare. They must have come up behind me while I sat against the fence post. It was surprising to think how quiet they must have been.

'They're just inquisitive,' said Dicky. 'They don't mean any harm.'

I tried to spot the one who'd been most inquisitive of all: she seemed to have melted back into the herd.

'Mooo?' I said to the line of black and white faces, but none of them replied.

And then, from behind us: 'Dicky.'

We turned.

'Dick, for short,' put in Maggot Boy. 'Or Sick.' He sniggered.

'*Dicky*,' Max said again.

Dicky said nothing and nor did I.

'You never said your name was Dicky,' Max said. 'You should've. It's a good name: good for *you*.'

When Max wasn't speaking it seemed very quiet. Still, too. Nobody moved – except, now, Max, who laid down Dicky's rod and stood up.

'*Why* didn't you say your name was Dicky? Shy, were you? Tell you what, come here and whisper the reason now.'

Dicky moved forward. I knew he was dead scared. Beside him, I went forward, too. I knew all this was my fault.

I had to step over the roach in the sandwich box. There it lay, waiting. Not helpless and tame, I knew now.

We stood before Max. I pressed close against Dicky. Max kept his eyes on Dicky. 'Get her away,' he said – meaning me. 'Little girlies should play with their dolls.'

But Dicky said nothing. He was too scared to speak. The only sound at that moment was the quiet, quiet ripple, from behind Max, of the river. Max reached out to shove me aside. The river whispered. I don't know whether he'd even touched me, when suddenly I pushed him in.

He looked surprised. As he toppled, arms

flailing, he looked at me and he looked *surprised*. Then he hit the water.

After that, there was lots of noise. Splashing, of course, and shouting and swearing. Max had got tangled with Maggot Boy's line, and Maggot Boy was trying to reel it in; Max was shrieking that the hook was in his bum, and Maggot Boy was cackling that they'd catch a whale with that. The river was deep and quite reedy where Max was, but he was lunging his way to the bank. The bank was steep just there, with no foot-holds, but Maggot Boy would soon pull him out.

And then we'd be for it.

'Quick, Charlie,' Dicky yelled. 'Run!' He snatched up his rod and made for our bikes.

I started to run and then stopped. Turned back. Max hadn't yet reached the bank.

I ran to the sandwich box. Picked it up – carefully, steadily – in both hands. Max thrust his hand towards Maggot Boy's outstretched one, but the two didn't touch: Max still wasn't quite close enough.

Steady, steady, I told myself. I felt the roach shudder. *Don't start thrashing, please.* And I raised up the box like some trophy I'd won. Steadily, up above my head. And then flung it.

Over the heads of the boys. To the river.

SSHLOCK! One thrash and, in mid-air, the plastic prison was flicked away. For a moment a spearhead hung in the sky, then the fish was dropping, flexing wildly, falling back to the water.

'Charlie!' screamed Dicky. 'Come *on*!' Max had got to the bank.

I ran.

Pushing our bikes up the rough farm track – pounding into potholes, rattling over ruts – I thought mine was going to buck out of my hands. Or fall to pieces. But it did neither. Dicky kept beside me – though he could have gone much faster.

We came to the bridleway, mounted our bikes. Still Dicky didn't pull ahead.

We came to the road, looked left, looked right.

Looked back. No one in sight.

Dicky laughed.

And I knew he'd never go there again.

There were plenty of other places to fish.

Children of Wax

Alexander McCall Smith
Illustrated by Ruthine Burton

Not far from the hills of the Matopos there lived a family whose children were made out of wax. The mother and the father in this family were exactly the same as everyone else, but for some reason their children had turned out to be made of wax.

At first this caused them great sorrow, and they wondered who had put such a spell on them, but later they became quite accustomed to this state of affairs and grew to love their children dearly.

It was easy for the parents to love the wax children. While other children might fight among themselves or forget to do their duty, wax children were always well-behaved and never fought with one another. They were also hard workers, one wax child being able to do the work of at least two ordinary children.

The only real problem which the wax children gave was that people had to avoid making fires too close to them, and of course they also had to work only at night. If they worked during the day, when the sun was hot, the wax children would melt.

To keep them out of the sun, their father made the wax children a dark hut that had no windows. During the day no rays of the sun could penetrate into the gloom of this hut, and so the wax children were quite safe. Then, when the sun had gone down, the children would come out of their dark hut and begin their work. They tended the crops and watched over the cattle, just as ordinary children did during the daytime.

There was one wax child, Ngwabi, who used to talk about what it was like during the day.

'We can never know what the world is like,' he said to his brothers and sisters. 'When we come out of our hut everything is quite dark and we see so little.'

Ngwabi's brothers and sisters knew that

153

what he said was right, but they accepted they would never know what the world looked like. There were other things that they had which the other children did not have, and they contented themselves with these. They knew, for instance, that other children felt pain: wax children never experienced pain, and for this they were grateful.

But poor Ngwabi still longed to see the world. In his dreams he saw the hills in the distance and watched the clouds that brought rain. He saw paths that led this way and that through the bush, and he longed to be able to follow them. But that was something that a wax child could never do, as it was far too dangerous to follow such paths in the night-time.

As he grew older, this desire of Ngwabi's

to see what the world was really like when the sun was up grew stronger and stronger. At last he was unable to contain it any more and he ran out of the hut one day when the sun was riding high in the sky and all about there was light and more light. The other children screamed, and some of them tried to grab at him as he left the hut, but they failed to stop their brother and he was gone.

Of course he could not last long in such heat. The sun burned down on Ngwabi and before he had taken more than a few steps he felt all the strength drain from his limbs. Crying out to his brothers and sisters, he fell to the ground and was soon nothing more than a pool of wax in the dust. Inside the hut, afraid to leave its darkness, the other wax children wept for their melted brother.

When night came, the children left their hut and went to the spot where Ngwabi had fallen. Picking up the wax, they went to a special place they knew and there Ngwabi's eldest sister made the wax into a bird. It was a bird with great wings, and for feathers they put a covering of leaves from the trees that grew there. These leaves would protect the wax from the sun so that it would not melt when it became day.

After they had finished their task, they told their parents what had happened. The man and woman wept, and each of them kissed the wax model of a bird. Then they set it upon a rock that stood before the wax children's hut.

The wax children did not work that night. At dawn they were all in their hut, peering through a small crack that there was in the wall. As the light came up over the hills, it made the wax bird seem pink with fire. Then, as the sun itself rose over the fields, the great bird which they had made suddenly moved its wings and launched itself into the air. Soon it was high above the ground, circling over the children's hut. A few minutes later it was gone, and the children knew that their brother was happy at last.

The Snag

Ted Hughes
Illustrated by Rachael Saunders

Right from the beginning Eel was grey. And his wife was grey. And his children were grey.

They lived in the bed of the river under a stone. There they lay, loosely folded together, Eel and his wife, and two of his children.

They breathed, and they waited, under a big stone.

Eel could peer out. He saw the water insects skittering about over the gravel, and sometimes swimming up through the water, to disappear through a ring of ripples. Where did they go?

He saw the bellies of the Trout, the Dace, the Minnows, and one Salmon, hovering in the current, or resting on the points of the stones on the river bed, their fins astir endlessly.

All day he lay under the dark stone.

But at night, when the sun went behind the wood, and the river grew suddenly dark, he slipped out. His wife and his two children followed him. Their noses were keener than any Dog's. They could smell every insect. They rootled in the gravel of the river pool, nipping up the insects.

But wherever he went over the river bed, he heard the cry: 'Here comes the grey snake! Look out for the grey snake! The grey snake is out! Watch for your babies!'

The fish could see him. Even in the dark, the fish with their luminous eyes could see him very well. They darted close, to see him better.

'Here he is!' piped a Trout, in a thin treble voice. 'He's coming upstream. Horrible eyes is coming upstream.'

And then: 'Here he is!' chattered the Minnows. 'He's turning back downstream.'

Wherever he moved, the fish kept up their

cries: 'Here's the grey snake now. Here he comes! Watch your babies!'

Eel pretended not to care. He poked his nose under the pebbles, picking out the insects. But the endless pestering got on his nerves. And his two children were frightened. 'We're not snakes,' he would shout. 'We may be grey, but we're fish.'

Then all the fish began to laugh, so the river pool shook. 'Fish are silver,' they cried. 'Or green, or gold, or speckled, with pinky fins. Fish are beautiful. Fish have scales. They are shaped like fish. But you are grey. You have no scales. And you are a snake. Snake! Snake! Snake!'

They would begin to chant it all together, opening and closing their mouths. And Eel and his wife and children would finally glide back under their stone and lie hidden.

In a few minutes the fish would forget about them.

If there had been anywhere else to go, Eel would have gone there, to escape the fish of that pool. Once he did take his wife downstream, to a much bigger, deeper pool. But that was worse. Nearly thirty big Salmon lay there, as well as many Trout and Dace and Minnows. The Salmon had shattering voices. They were used to calling to each other out on the stormy high seas. And now when Eel came slithering from under his stone, when night fell, a deafening chorus met him:

'Here comes the grey snake. Here he comes to eat your children. Here he comes. Watch out!'

And all the time he was hunting they kept it up: 'Go home, grey snake! Go home, grey snake!'

Finally Eel led his family back to the smaller pool, where there was only one Salmon.

His two children stopped going out at night. They lay curled up under the stone, crying. 'What are we?' they sobbed. 'Are we really grey snakes? If we aren't fish, what are we?'

Eel scowled and tried to comfort them. But he couldn't help worrying. 'What if I am a grey snake, after all? How can I prove I'm a fish?'

Eel had only one friend, a Lamprey. Lamprey was quite like Eel, but he was so ugly he didn't worry about anything. 'I know I'm a horror,' he would say. 'But so what? Being ugly makes you smart.'

One day this Lamprey said to Eel: 'I know a fortune-teller. She could tell you what you are. Why don't you ask her?'

Eel reared up like a swan. 'A Fortune-teller,' he cried. 'Why didn't you tell me?'

'I've told you,' said Lamprey.

This Fortune-teller, it turned out, was the new moon. 'How can the new moon tell fortunes?' asked Eel.

'She tells fortunes only for a few minutes each day,' explained Lamprey. 'You have to get to her just as she touches the sea's edge, going down. Then she tells fortunes until she sinks out of sight. You have to listen very carefully. You don't hear her with your ears. You hear her with your thoughts.'

'Let's go,' said Eel. And he wanted to set off that minute downstream, but Lamprey checked him.

'Take a witness,' said Lamprey.

'A witness?' asked Eel. 'What for?'

'Unless you have a witness to what the new moon says, the fish will never believe you. Take the Salmon.'

The Salmon was so sure the new moon would tell Eel he was really a snake, and not a fish at all, that he was eager to come. 'I want to hear that,' he cried. 'I'll bring the truth back. Then you can stay out there in the sea, you needn't come back at all. It's the truth we want, not you.'

So they set off. It was quite a journey, getting to the new moon. But finally Eel got there, with Lamprey beside him, to keep his spirits up, and, skulking behind, the Salmon.

The new moon was actually a smile without a face. It lay on the sea's rim like a face on a pillow. And the Smile smiled as Eel told his problem. It smiled as it sank slowly.

'You are a fish,' said the Smile. 'Not only are you a fish. You are a fish that God made for himself. God made you for himself.'

'Me?' cried Eel. 'God made me for himself? Why?'

'Because,' said the Smile, 'you are the sweetest of all the fish.'

The Salmon slammed the water with his tail. He'd always thought he was the sweetest. This was bad news on top of bad news.

'Say that again,' cried the Eel.

'You are the sweetest of all the fish,' said

the Smile. It spoke so loud the whole sea chimed like a gong with the words.

Eel didn't know what to say. 'Thank you,' he stammered. 'Oh, thank you.' He was thinking how his children would jump up and down, as much as they could under their rock, when he told them this.

'But,' said the Smile, as it sank. It seemed to be sinking faster and faster. There was only a little horn of light left, a little bright thorn, sticking above the sea.

'But?' cried the Eel. 'But what?'

'There's a snag,' said the Smile, and vanished.

'What snag? What's the snag?' cried Eel.

But the Smile had gone. The sea looked darker and colder. A shoal of Flying Fish burst upwards with a shivering laugh, and splashed back in again.

Still, Eel had what he wanted. And both Lamprey and Salmon were witnesses. Salmon had already gone, furious, as Eel and Lamprey set off home.

Back in the pool, Eel called all the fish together and told them exactly what had been said. 'I am a fish,' he said. 'Not only that, I am God's favourite fish. God made me for himself. Because among all the fish, I am the sweetest.'

'It is true,' said the Lamprey. 'I was there.'

'Yes,' said the Salmon. 'Perhaps she did say that. But what did she mean? That's what I'd like to know. What did she mean?'

Even so, the fish were impressed. They didn't like it, but they were impressed. And from that moment, Eel and his wife and children surged about the pool throughout the day as well as the night. 'Make way for God's own fish,' he would shout, and butt the Salmon. 'Make way for the sweetest!'

The fish didn't know what to do. The story soon got about. The Heron and the Kingfisher told it to the birds. The Otter told it to the animals. A crowd of them came to Man, and told him what had happened.

Man, who was drinking very sour cider, which he had just made out of crab-apples, pondered.

'What,' he said finally, 'does the Eel mean by sweetest? How sweetest? Sweetest what? Sweetest nature?'

All the creatures became thoughtful. Then they became wildly excited.

'Man's got it!' they cried. 'What does the horrible Eel mean by sweetest? Sweetest how?'

The fish came crowding around Eel and his family. 'Sweetest what?' they shouted. 'How are you sweetest? Come and prove you're the sweetest! You and your hideous infants. You and your goblin wife.'

'It's a riddle,' said the Salmon. 'The new moon posed a riddle. What does sweetest mean?'

'We are sweeter than any Eel,' cried the flowers. And the wild roses and the honeysuckles poured their perfumes over the river.

'And we are sweeter than any dumb Eel,' cried the Thrushes, the Blackbirds, the Robins, the Wrens, and they poured out their brilliant songs over the river.

'And my children are the sweetest of all the animals,' cried the Otter, holding up its kittens.

'They are not,' cried the Sheep, and she butted forward her two Lambs.

'No, they are not,' cried the Fox, suddenly standing there with a woolly cub.

'Among the fish,' cried the Eel. 'That's what she said. I am the sweetest among the fish. Who cares about perfumes? Who wants to smell? And who cares about song? What counts is the thought. And who cares about fluffy darlings? The Otter grows up to murder Eels. The Lamb grows up to butcher the flowers. The Fox-cub grows up to murder the Mice. What sort of sweetness is that? No. My sweetness is the real sweetness, the sort that God loves best.'

'Taste?' asked Man. 'That leaves only taste.'

Eel would have blinked, if he had had eyelids. Taste? He hadn't thought of that.

'That's it!' shouted the fish, sticking their heads out of the water. 'Taste! Cook us and eat us, see who's the sweetest. Taste us all. Taste us all!'

Eel felt suddenly afraid. Who was going to taste him? Was Man going to cook him? But the fish were shouting to Man: 'You can eat one of each of us. And then eat Eel as well, and then you can judge. Here we are. Here we are.'

The fish were quite ready to let one of each kind of them be eaten so long as it meant that Eel too would be eaten.

'No,' cried Eel. 'Wait.'

But fish were jumping ashore. One Trout, one Dace, one Minnow, and even that Salmon – he too was offering himself. All to get the Eel killed and eaten!

Eel twisted round and fled. But the Otter plunged in after him. And in the swirling chase, the Otter grabbed Eel's wife. She was much bigger than Eel anyway.

Eel coiled under the stone with his two children. He couldn't believe it. The oven was glowing, the fish were frying. And his wife too! It was terrible! But all he could do was stare and feel helpless.

And Man and Woman were already testing, with dainty forks and thin slices of buttered brown bread.

They didn't like Dace at all. He tasted of mud. The Minnow was quite nice – but peculiar. The Trout was fairly good – but a little too watery. He needed lemon and – and – something. And the Salmon – the Salmon, now! Well, the Salmon seemed just about the most wonderful thing possible – till they tasted Eel.

Woman uttered a cry and almost dropped her fork. Tears came into her eyes and she stared at Man.

'Was there ever anything so delicious!' she gasped. 'So sweet! So sweet!'

Man rested his brow on his hand.

'How have we lived so long,' he said, 'and not realised what gorgeous goodies lay down there, under the river stones? How could anything be sweeter than this Eel?'

'Eel!' he shouted. 'You have won. God is right again. You are the sweetest!'

Eel heard and trembled. And he shrank back under the stone, deeper into the dark, when he heard Man say: 'Bring me another!'

Otter came swirling down through the

current. Otter was working for Man. Eel and his two children shot downstream. But one had to be hindmost. One of the children. And when Eel looked round, only one of his children was following.

And as they slipped and squirmed down through the shallows, among the stones, towards the next pool below, the Heron peered down out of heaven and – *Szwack*! The other Eel-child was twisting in the Heron's long bill. The Heron too was working for Man.

But the Eels were so sweet, neither Otter nor Heron could resist eating them on the spot. From that moment, the Otter hid from Man and spent all his time hunting more Eels – for himself. And from that moment Heron was afraid of Man – flapping up and reeling away with a panicky 'Aaaark' – only to land somewhere else where he could go on hunting Eels – for himself. Neither Otter nor Heron wanted to hand over what they caught – Eels were much too sweet!

But Eel himself hid from all of them. He oiled his body, to make it hard to grip. And whenever he sees the slightest glow of light he hides deeper under the stones, or deeper into the mud. He thinks it is Man searching for him. Or he thinks it is the point of the moon sinking and he suddenly remembers THE SNAG.

Yes, the snag.

Hey, Danny!

Robin Klein
Illustrated by Ruthine Burton

'Right,' said Danny's mother sternly. 'That school bag cost ten pounds. You can just save up your pocket money to buy another one. How could you possibly lose a big school bag, anyhow?'

'Dunno,' said Danny. 'I just bunged in some

empty bottles to take back to the milkbar, and I was sort of swinging it round by the handles coming home, and it sort of fell over that culvert thing down on to a lorry on the motorway.'

'And you forgot to write your name and phone number in it as I told you to,' said Mrs Hillerey. 'Well, you'll just have to use my blue weekend bag till you save up enough pocket money to replace the old one. And no arguments!'

Danny went and got the blue bag from the hall cupboard and looked at it.

The bag was not just blue; it was a vivid, clear, electric blue, like a flash of lightning. The regulation colour for schoolbags at his school was a khaki-olive-brown, inside and out, which didn't show stains from when your can of Coke leaked, or when you left your salami sandwiches uneaten and forgot about them for a month.

'I can't take this bag to school,' said Danny. 'Not one this colour. Can't I take my books and stuff in one of those green plastic rubbish bags?'

'Certainly not!' said Mrs Hillerey.

On Monday at the bus stop, the kids all stared at the blue bag.

'Hey,' said Jim, who was supposed to be his mate. 'That looks like one of those bags girls take to ballet classes.'

'Hey, Danny, you got one of those frilly dresses in there?' asked Spike.

'Aw, belt up, can't you?' said Danny miserably. On the bus the stirring increased as more and more kids got on. It was a very long trip for Danny. It actually took only twenty minutes – when you had an ordinary brown schoolbag and not a great hunk of sky to carry round with you. Every time anyone spoke to him they called him 'Little Boy Blue'.

'It matches his lovely blue eyes,' said one kid.

'Maybe he's got a little blue trike with training wheels too,' said another kid.

'Hey, Danny, why didn't you wear some nice blue ribbons in your hair?'

When Danny got off the bus he made a dash for his classroom and shoved the bag under his desk. First period they had Miss Reynolds, and when she was marking the register she looked along the aisle and saw Danny's bag and said, 'That's a very elegant bag you have there, Danny.'

Everyone else looked round and saw the blue bag and began carrying on. Danny kept a dignified silence, and after five minutes Miss Reynolds made them stop singing 'A life on the Ocean Waves'. But all through maths and English, heads kept turning round to grin at Danny and his radiantly blue bag.

At break he sneaked into the art room and mixed poster paints into a shade of khaki-olive-brown which he rubbed over his bag with his hankie. When the bell rang he had a grey handkerchief, but the bag was still a clear and innocent blue. 'Darn thing,' Danny muttered in disgust. 'Must be made of some kind of special waterproof atomic material. Nothing sticks to it.'

'What are you doing in the art room, Daniel?' asked Miss Reynolds. 'And what is that terrible painty mess?'

'I was just painting a Zodiac sign on my bag,' said Danny.

'I wish you boys wouldn't write things all over your good school bags. Clean up that mess, Danny, and go to your next lesson.'

But Danny said he was feeling sick and could he please lie down in the sick bay for a while. He sneaked his blue bag in with him, and found the key to the first-aid box and looked inside for something that would turn bright blue bags brown. There was a little bottle of brown lotion, so Danny tipped the whole lot on to cotton wool and scrubbed it into the surface of the bag. But the lotion just ran off the bag and went all over his hands and the bench top in the sick bay.

'Danny Hillerey!' said the school secretary. 'You know very well that no pupil is allowed to unlock the first-aid box. What on earth are you doing?'

'Sorry,' said Danny. 'Just looking for some liver salts.'

'I think you'd better sit quietly out in the fresh air if you feel sick,' Mrs Adams said suspiciously. 'And who owns that peculiar-looking blue bag?'

'It belongs in the sports equipment shed,' said Danny. 'It's got measuring tapes and stuff in it. Blue's our house colour.'

He went and sat outside with the bag shoved under the seat and looked at it and despaired. Kids from his class started going down to the oval for games, and they started in on him again.

Danny glared and said 'Get lost' and 'Drop dead'. Then Miss Reynolds came along and made him go down to the oval with the others.

On the way there Danny sloshed the blue bag in a puddle of mud – but nothing happened, the blue became shinier, if anything. He also tried grass stains under the sprinkler, which had the same effect. Among the line-up of khaki-olive-brown bags, his blue one was as conspicuous as a Clydesdale horse in a herd of small ponies.

'Hey, Danny, what time's your tap dancing lesson?' said the kids.

'Hey, Danny, where did you get that knitting bag? I want to buy one for my aunty.'

'Hey, Danny, when did you join the Bluebell marching girls' squad?'

Finally Danny had had enough.

'This bag's very valuable, if you want to know,' he said.

'Rubbish,' everyone scoffed. 'It's just an ordinary old vinyl bag.'

'I had to beg my mum to let me bring that bag to school,' said Danny. 'It took some doing, I can tell you. Usually she won't let it out of the house.'

'Why?' demanded everyone. 'What's so special about it?'

Danny grabbed his bag and wiped off the traces of mud and poster paint and brown lotion and grass stains. The bag was stained inside where all that had seeped in through the seams and the zip, and it would take some explaining when his mother noticed it. (Which she would, next time she went to spend the weekend at Grandma's.) There was her name inside, E. Hillerey, in big neat letters. E for Enid.

'Well,' said Danny, 'that bag belonged to . . . well, if you really want to know, it went along on that expedition up Mount Everest.'

Everyone jeered.

'It did so,' said Danny. 'Look, Sir Edmund Hillary, there's his name printed right there inside. And there's a reason it's this funny colour. So it wouldn't get lost in the snow. It was the bag Sir Edmund Hillary carried that flag in they stuck up on top of Mount Everest. But I'm not going to bring it to school any more if all you can do is poke fun at the colour.'

Everyone went all quiet and respectful.

'Wow,' said Jeff in an awed voice, and he touched the letters that Danny's mother had written with a laundry-marking pencil.

'Gosh,' said Mark. 'We never knew you were related to that Sir Edmund Hillary.'

Danny looked modest. 'We're only distantly related,' he admitted. 'He's my dad's second cousin.'

'Hey, Danny, can I hold it on the bus? I'll be really careful with it.'

'Hey, Danny, can I have a turn when you bring it to school tomorrow?'

'I'll charge you ten pence a go,' said Danny.

'That's fair, for a bag that went up to the top of Mount Everest.'

'Ten pence a kid,' he calculated. 'One hundred kids at ten pence a turn, ten pounds.

A new brown school bag. And with a bit of luck, I'll earn all that before someone checks up in the library and finds out Sir Edmund Hillary's name's spelt differently!'

The Bakerloo Flea

Michael Rosen
Illustrated by Rachael Saunders

Not long ago I was in a pub round the Elephant and Castle, and I got talking to a woman, an oldish woman. And we were talking about this and that, and she said she used to be a cleaner down the Underground. I didn't know, but it seems as if every night after the last tube, they switch the electric current off and teams of night-cleaners go through the Underground, along the tunnels, cleaning up all the muck, rubbish, fag ends and stuff that we chuck on to the lines. They sweep out between the lines on one station, and then, in a gang of about six or seven, walk on to the next station along the lines in the tunnels.

Anyway this woman (I don't know her name), she says to me:

'Did you ever hear talk of the Bakerloo flea?'

'Bakerloo flea?' I said. 'No, no, never.'

'Well,' she said, 'you know there are rats down there – down the Underground? Hundreds of 'em. And the thing is,' she said, 'is that some of them have grown enormous. Huge great big things.'

'I've heard of them,' I said. 'Super rats.'

'Right,' she says. 'Now you tell me,' she says, 'what lives on rats? Fleas, right? Fleas. So – the bigger the rats the bigger the fleas. Stands to reason. These rats, they feed on all the old garbage that people throw down on the lines. It's amazing what people throw away, you know.'

She told me they found a steak down there once, lipstick, a bowler hat, beads, a box of eggs and hundreds and hundreds of sweets – especially Maltesers and those balls of bubble gum you get out of slot machines.

Anyway, the rats eat these, get big, and it seems that one day they were working the Bakerloo Line – Elephant and Castle to Paddington – and just before Baker Street one of the women in the gang was looking ahead, and she screamed out:

'Look – look – what's that?' Up in front was a great, grey, spiky thing with huge hairy legs and big jaws. It was as big as a big dog – bigger.

And the moment she screamed, it jumped away from them, making a sort of grating, scraping noise. Well, they were scared stiff. Scared stiff. But they had to finish the job, so they carried on up the line to Paddington. But they didn't see it again that night or the next, or the next.

Some of them thought they'd imagined it, because it can get very spooky down there. They sing and shout a lot, she told me, and tell saucy jokes, not fit for my ears.

Anyway, about a fortnight later, at the same place – just before Baker Street on the Bakerloo Line – suddenly one of them looks up and there it was again. A great, big, grey, spiky thing with long legs and big jaws.

'It's a flea, sure to God, it's a flea,' one of them said.

The moment it heard this, again it jumped. Again, they heard this scraping, grating sound, and it disappeared down the tunnel – in the dark. They walked on, Baker Street, Marylebone, Edgware Road, to Paddington. Nothing.

Anyway – this time they had a meeting. They decided it *was* a flea, a gigantic flea, and it must have grown up from a family of fleas that had lived for years and years growing bigger and bigger, sucking the blood of all the fat rats down there.

So they decided that it was time to tell one of the high-ups in London Transport, or they wouldn't go down there any more.

For a start-off, no one'd believe them.

'Just a gang of women seeing things in the dark,' the supervisor said.

Right! One of them had a bright idea. She said:

'I'll tell you what we'll do – we'll tell them that we're coming out on strike, and we'll tell the papers about the flea, the Bakerloo flea. It'll be a huge scandal – no one'll dare go by tube, it'll be a national scandal.'

So they threatened the manager with this, and this time the high-ups really moved. They were so scared the story might get out, and they'd be blamed, and one of them would lose his job.

So for a start they stopped all cleaning on the Bakerloo line, and one of the high-ups went down the tunnel with the women. You can just see it, can't you? Four in the morning, a gang of six women with feather dusters, and one of the bowler hat and briefcase brigade walking down the tunnel on the hunt for the Bakerloo flea. Sounded incredible to me.

Anyway, it seems as if they came round that same corner just before Baker Street and the woman had gone quiet and the bloke was saying: 'If this is a hoax, if this is a trick . . .' when they heard that awful, hollow, scraping noise.

At first they couldn't see it, but then – there it was – not *between* the lines this time – *on* the lines – a gigantic flea. No question, that's what it was.

Well, he took one look at it, and next moment he was backing off.

'Back, ladies, back. Back, ladies!'

Of course *he* was more scared than they were. Terrified. But he was even more terrified when one of the women let out this scream. Not because *she* was scared, but to scare off the flea. And it worked. It jumped. Right out of sight.

Well, there was no carrying on up the line that night.

'Back, ladies, back,' was all he could say, and back they went.

Next thing they knew, they were all called into an office with a carpet and the Queen on the wall. And there was a whole gang of these men.

First thing, one of them says, they weren't to let anyone know of this, no one at all must ever hear of what they had all seen. There was no point in letting a panic develop. Anyway, next he says:

'We haven't let the grass grow under our feet. We've got a scientist with us.'

And then the scientist, he says:

'I've got this powder. Deadly flea powder. All you need to do is spread this up and down the Bakerloo Line, and there'll be no more trouble with this flea thing.'

Well, the woman in the pub – I never found out her name – said:

'So who's going to spread this stuff about down there? The army?'

'No,' the man said. 'We don't see any need for that. You,' he says, 'you.'

'So there's a fine one,' the woman said to me. 'First of all they said it was just a bunch of women afraid of the dark, then they send

Tarzan in pinstripes down there and he can't get out fast enough, and now it's us that has to spread this flea powder.

'Well,' she said, 'we knew it wouldn't be any good anyway. Flea powder never is.' They took it down there, threw it about between Regent's Park and Baker Street and Edgware Road – while up above, in the big houses, ambassadors from all over the world slept soundly in their beds. They told them not to go down for a week, and not to breathe a word of it to anyone.

'They were more scared of a story in the papers than we were of the flea,' she said.

It hadn't attacked anyone, no one had seen it there in daytime, so down they went. But there it was again – sitting there just before Baker Street, with some of the powder sticking to the hairs on its legs. But this time, instead of hopping away down the line, it turned and faced them. They turned and ran, and then it leapt. It leapt at the women, and they ran back down the tunnel to Regent's Park. This great, grey flea was trying to get at them.

'We screamed,' she said, 'we really screamed, but it was after us, 'cos you see, that damned flea powder hadn't killed the flea – it had killed the rats. It was starving for fresh blood. Probably *mad* for blood, by now,' she said. 'We ran and ran and the flea was hopping – but it was hitting the roof of the tunnel, it was so mad to get at us. There was this terrible scraping sound of its shell on the roof of the tunnel, and it'd fall back on to the lines. So we could move faster than it. We rushed back to Regent's Park, and calls went up and down the line and all over the system to lock the gates on every station and seal the system. Seal off the Underground system of London. Well, it was about four o'clock – two hours to go before a million people would be down there.

'What were they going to do? Upstairs in the office they were in a blind panic. They could've done something about it earlier, instead of fobbing us off. They couldn't call in the army without telling the Minister, and if they told the Minister, he'd tell the Prime Minister, and all the high-ups would get the sack. So they had this plan to turn the current on, and run the maintenance train at high speed through the tunnel from Paddington to the Elephant and Castle, in the hope that it would get killed beneath the wheels of the train, or smashed against the buffers at the Elephant.

'They did it. They sent it through. Of course *that* didn't work. We knew it wouldn't work. Anyone that's lived with a flea knows you can't squash fleas – you've got to crack 'em. They're hard, rock hard.

'After the maintenance man ran the maintenance train through, they went down to the gates at Regent's Park, and they stood and listened, and from down below they could hear the grating, scraping noise of its shell on its legs. Of course, it was obvious now why it had stuck to this stretch of the line all the time. Some of the juiciest rubbish was in the bins round those posh parts, so you got the biggest rats, so that was where you got the great Bakerloo flea.

'So now they had less than two hours to get rid of the flea, or leave it for a day and run the risk of letting a million people down into the tunnels to face a flea, starving, starving for blood, or shutting the whole system down and telling everyone to go by bus.

'Well, you know what happened?' she said. '*We* did it. *We* got rid of it.'

'You did?'

'Yes, we did it. Vera's old man worked on the dustcarts for Camden council. She knew how to kill the flea. It was Vera's plan that what we'd do was go down, actually down on to the line at Oxford Circus with dustbin lids, banging them with brushes and broom handles, and drive the flea back up the line to Queen's Park where the Bakerloo Line comes out of the tunnel into the open air. And at Queen's Park, Vera's old man and his gang would have a couple of carts backed up into the tunnel. And that's what we did. We got driven to Vera's place to get her old man up, on to his mates' places to get them up, then they went to the council builders' yard to get boards, builders' planks. We got the lids off the bins, and down we went. Oxford Circus, Regent's Park, Baker Street, Marylebone, Edgware Road, Paddington and we shouted and we banged, and we banged and we shouted every step of the way.

'We saw it just once at Edgware Road waiting for us, but we walked together, holding the lids up in front of us like shields, and it was as if it knew it couldn't get at us this time, 'cos it turned – it had just room to turn in the tunnel – and as we came up to Queen's Park still banging and shouting, it leapt – not at us, but at one of the carts. Alongside it was the other one, between the wheels were the boards, some of them stacked up to block off all the gaps. The flea was trapped between us with our lids and the back of the dustcarts. It leapt, it hit the roof of the tunnel, just like it did when it chased us. We shouted and banged. It leapt again. This time we had it. It was in the back of the dustcart.

We kept up the banging and the shouting. We got as near to the back of the dustcart as we could. We could see it there, every hair of its legs, and Vera shouts:

"Turn it on, Bob, turn it on," and Bob turned on the masher (they call it The Shark), in the back of his cart. And it bit into the back of that flea like giant nails crunching through eggshells. The smell was revolting. Bit by bit, the flea was dragged into the cart. We could see it as it went: first its body, then its legs. I'll never forget the sight of those huge hairy legs twitching about in the back of Bob's cart, Vera shouting:

"You've got him, love, you've got him!"

He had, too. That was that. That was the end of the Bakerloo flea. But do you know, when we got up to the top, that load from head office were there. They were crying, crying out of relief, crying their eyes out. Twenty minutes later, hundreds and thousands of people were down there, off to work, none the wiser. They didn't know about any flea, any Bakerloo flea. They don't even know we go down there every night cleaning up their mess for them. Of course, head office made us promise never to breathe a word of it. We promised.

Vera said: "What's it worth to you?"

He said: "Your honour. Your word. And your word's your honour."

And they gave us a week's extra holiday tagged on to August Bank Holiday that year.'

She told me I was the first person she'd ever told the story to, and told me never to tell anyone. The scandal would be terrible. I don't know whether to believe her or not.

Storm Children

Pauline Hill
Illustrated by Rachael Saunders

I'm not one to swank, but I reckon I'm pretty good at lots of things. Not sums and spelling and Scottish dancing (my legs go wrong in the twisty bits) . . . but, well, scrambling eggs, for instance, and sewing the hem of my sister's dress when it comes undone (as it does most times she comes home after chasing in the field with the Baker kids – they always find the filthiest places to skip and slide in). What's more, I'm always first up the ropes in the gym, and I finish first with my paper round, if old Mrs Hennessey doesn't pop out in her red dressing-gown for a yarn.

There's no end to the things I *can* do. Sometimes when I feel sulky, I'll hunt out the posh writing-pad Aunt Cynthia gave me for Christmas and my red felt-tip, the one that I keep for recording Riotous Events, and make a list of everything I *can* do, just to cheer myself up. Loads of things.

1. *I'm the only one on our street who's actually grown hollyhocks*
2. *And great big sunflowers so that I can*

feed Mrs Pankhurst's hens with the seeds, and Mrs Pankhurst sometimes gives me new-laid eggs, so that's a bonus

3. *And I'm always the first to find snowdrops in the woods*

4. *And violets*

5. *And last autumn I made ten jars of blackberry jam from blackberries I picked in the woods*

6. *And I brush my dog Shaggy's coat till it glistens like spun silk, and he won 1st prize at the Dog Show*

7. *And some kids haven't even got dogs they can take for walks in the fields and go down to the market to buy biscuits for.*

But there's one thing that always really frightened me. More than ghosts. More than witches. More than little green men from Outer Space. I didn't tell anyone about it, because looking at me you wouldn't think I was frightened of anything, ever. But I couldn't get through a thunderstorm without shivering and trembling and getting in a right old tizz. Once I even wet my pants, I was so scared. But I kept the fear to myself mostly. It's better not to tell folks what you're afraid of; they find out soon enough.

It really was strange how I came to be cured of thunderstorms. Part of it's to do with Mr Trenchard, my history teacher. He's mad on old buildings, monuments, old crumbly houses and spooky castles. Once he took our class to peer at a Roman wall, all broken away and powdery with beetles crawling all over. I didn't think much of it. My dad builds much better walls. I could've summoned up a faint glimmer of excitement if we'd actually seen Roman soldiers building it, but when I mentioned it to Mr Trenchard he seemed a bit put out. 'Don't be stupid, Tracey. Try to use the few brains you've got, child!' Which was a bit off. I can't stand grown-ups who call me 'child'.

We had to do one of those questionnaires about the Roman wall. I got all the answers from Peter Green. My marks were quite high in that questionnaire, it certainly surprised Mr Trenchard. But I did like the stories he told us about our town in wartime. My mum won't ever tell me about the war; she says it's better forgotten; but Mr Trenchard keeps bits of old planes in his garage, and lets kids polish them, and he'll sometimes give out Mars Bars too.

He's got a photo of himself in RAF uniform when he was a pilot in the Battle of Britain; he looked quite handsome in those days. One September night in 1940 his squadron shot down an enemy plane over Devil's Finger, just a few miles away. The pilot baled out, over the woods, but his parachute got caught in the branches of a tree, and he was killed.

Well, this year, we had a half-day holiday in September because the vicar said we'd worked so hard bringing in the stuff for Harvest Festival (HP Sauce and conkers was what soppy Jenkins offered) and he wanted us to enjoy the warm weather before winter set in. Shaggy was waiting when I got home after school dinner – mince and salad, I ask you – and we set off towards the woods.

Lots of deep blue sky, bright golden

sunshine on the stubble fields, and Shaggy belting off after imaginary rabbits in the hedgerows. I love walking. Shaggy likes walking too. I've never known a dog who doesn't. So we must have gone four or five miles, and I hardly noticed the candy-floss clouds slipping off the edge of the sky.

But, stealthily, grey shadows crept up. I felt a plop of warm rain on my arm. And then . . . *Crack!* A heavy rumble. Fields lately friendly with sunshine became eerie, sinister. A flurry of wind lifted the leaves under the trees. Shaggy slunk close to me, tail between his legs, and licked my hand. 'It's all right, boy,' I comforted him, knowing that he was scared too. A dagger of lightning knifed across the sky. Thunder boomed overhead . . . rain cut down in solid sheets. Terror gripped me . . .

sheer blind panic! I must get away . . . anywhere, away from it all . . . Stumbling wildly, I ran on through the trees . . .

I came upon the farmhouse suddenly. ACRES BOTTOM FARM it said on the gate. One minute it wasn't there . . . the next it was.

I knew Mum wouldn't approve of me going up to a strange house, but I was so scared that I peered in at the window, and saw a big farm kitchen, with a wide and welcoming log fire roaring up the chimney – in September – and children, four, five, six of them, dancing in the firelight. I banged on the door, the children came rushing to open it, and a moment later Shaggy and I were inside the warm kitchen. It smelt apple-sweet and spicy with cinnamon. Rosy-cheeked, smiling, chattering like magpies, the children danced and clapped their hands. 'You found us. We knew you would!' said the tallest boy. 'We've been waiting so long.' They grabbed both my hands and pulled me into their frantic dance. They barely heard the claps of thunder, but I could see flashes of lightning through the windows. 'Don't you *love* storms?' asked one little girl.

'No . . . no. I don't.'

'But you *must!*' she cried. 'They're beautiful!'

Another deafening clap of thunder. The children laughed and laughed, dancing more furiously, forcing me to join in . . . making me dance and squeal and fight back against the storm with yells and laughs and dancing, dancing, dancing.

I don't know how long the storm lasted. It was over too soon for me. The fear inside me

suddenly snapped, and I'd never felt so wild and happy as I did that afternoon with the Storm Children.

It was well into evening, a calm and pastel sky after the fury. 'I must go now.'

'Promise to come again! Promise!'

'I will! I will!'

Mum had seen the gathering black clouds earlier, and had feared for me. She was on the afternoon shift at the clothing factory that week. When the storm broke she phoned Dad. He wasn't pleased. He was working nights, and hated being woken early, but Mum can be very persuasive. He uttered a few ripe words under his breath and went out looking for me. He hunted high and low, asked each soul he met . . . but returned home alone.

Mum panicked, of course, and he got the sharp end of her tongue. She'd come home early from the factory – she does fuss a lot. She rounded on him fiercely, demanding, 'Haven't you found her?' She always tosses her head haughtily when she's mad at Dad. Dad says it's her 'High Dudgeon' mood.

So when I'd said goodbye to the storm kids in the warm house and promised to come back with some blackberry jam for them to taste, I ran home to find Mum in a High Dudgeon. 'Well!' she glared crossly when I came in. 'A fine dance you've led us, young lady!'

'Hello, Mum.'

'Dad's been out looking for you! Where've you been, you naughty girl?'

'I sheltered in a house. When the storm came on. You know . . .'

'Of course I know how frightened you get. I used to be just the same! Which house was it? I've told you not to go into strange houses . . . not to talk to strangers . . .' She was white with anger. Dad says though she gets angry, her heart's in the right place.

'Oh, Mum,' I said, and gave her a hug.

'Which house?' Her tone softened. 'Which house, Tracey?'

'A farmhouse up near Devil's Finger.'

She didn't reply immediately. Then she said, 'There's no farmhouse up at Devil's Finger.' She looked sharply at Dad. 'Is there, Tom?'

'Well . . .' He picked up Mum's warning look. 'No. No farmhouse. There *used* to be . . .'

'You must know it,' I said. 'It's a farm called

223

Acres Bottom. Funny name, isn't it? Mum . . .
you all right?' She'd turned so pale that I
thought she was going to faint.

'I feel . . . a bit giddy,' she said. 'You know
how I get.'

After, when Mum had popped round next
door to see Mrs Pankhurst, Dad said, 'Your
mum's always been nervy, love. Ever since I
first knew her. She was only your age, then.
She still gets frightened sometimes.'

'By thunderstorms?'

'She's better than she used to be. But she
gets jumpy about all sorts of things.'

'That place. Acres Bottom . . .'

'There used to be a farm by that name. Back
in the War: 1940, it must have been – bombing
every blessed night. An enemy plane was shot
down near Devil's Finger. It crashed on the

224

farmhouse. Terrible disaster . . . all six kids killed in their beds.'

I gasped.

Dad went on, 'They say Acres Wood's haunted by the ghost of the German pilot. People reckon they've seen him on September evenings. All nonsense, of course, but you know how your mum gets.'

When Mum came back from next door, everything seemed different. I had suddenly grown older. I knew two things. I would never again be afraid of thunderstorms. And I knew that when I was Mum's age, I should never be afraid of things that still frightened her.

Months later, Mum asked casually, though her hands were clenched as she spoke, 'That day of the thunderstorm, Tracey. When you were in the woods that evening . . . you didn't see anything . . . ?'

I laughed gently. 'Oh, Mum,' I said. 'You've been listening to those silly stories about the ghost of the German pilot.'

'Well . . . ?'

'Of course not. That's all nonsense!'

But I never told her what I *had* seen, at Acres Bottom.

Blondin's Rainbow

Judith Vidal
Illustrated by Ruthine Burton

There was once a man called Blondin. He could walk higher and finer than any man in the world. So high and fine was his walking that he thought he would try the most difficult walk ever made, the highest and finest of any man. A wire was stretched tight and high, and a thousand feet long, above the waters of Niagara in the USA, the highest, deepest waterfall in the world. Blondin walks again!

For it was not the first time that Blondin had come to Niagara. He had been here before. He had done all that it was possible to do. He had wheeled wheelbarrows on his wire across the Falls; carried men on his back – men who trusted him; blind-folded without his eyes; on stilts that rocked as he walked. And finally, his most spectacular achievement of all, he had made and eaten an omelette there in the middle of his wire. He had carried his eggs and eaten them all. The crowds had gone wild with the joy and suspense.

And now here he was again. The hopes of the crowd were high, though their imagination failed. 'What would it be this time?' they asked themselves. 'What could he do that he had not already done?' Standing excitedly in the thin drizzle which had begun to fall they watched the arrival of the great man. 'A little older,' they said. 'A bit too old, perhaps, for this sort of thing. You have to know when to stop: quit whilst there's still time.' They shook their heads quietly, and raised quizzical eyebrows. Many of them were privately certain that he would not make it this time. He was fatter, more bulging in the calf, and his famous twirled moustache looked a little sad. But maybe he had learned a new trick or two, and they looked forward to some new and dazzling feat about to be performed above their heads, never believing for one minute that the wire alone could be enough, be it as high as never was. That, they thought, would be a cheat and disappointment. They hadn't travelled all those miles in the rain and early morning just for that. But they needn't worry, they decided. This was Blondin. And they cheered him as he stepped among them.

Indeed, all over Europe they had not ceased to cheer him. In circus rings, as high over the sawdust as it was possible to be, the lights above dazzling the eyes of those below, they had lifted up their faces to watch him, silent and intent. No one breathed. The children, or some of them, shut their eyes as he started out. Some stuffed their fists, tightly clenched, into their mouths to hold down a scream that might leak out. Others pushed their longest finger into each ear to keep out the crash. But there was never a crash. Every time the breathing which had stopped started again in a great sigh which rippled round the ring. The eyes opened, the fists and fingers came out to clap, and the new found voices cheered for all they were worth. 'Blondin! Blondin!'

They came from miles to see him in fairgrounds, circuses, music halls. His name was in the brightest lights: he headed every bill. But still, it seemed, for him it was not enough. 'I must get higher; stretch the wire finer.' He was never satisfied. He out-topped the biggest big top, and walked on his wire in the highest buildings men could offer. He even performed in magical palaces of glass over the heads of royalty, turned somersaults over them in the air in the soaring glass cage. Steadily and elegantly he walked and performed. His precarious balance looked like security to those who watched from below. They marvelled, and praised him all over the world. His life history appeared in the newspapers. They made up songs about him and sold them on the streets. And so he had finally come to Niagara to dance for them on his wire; to amaze and startle them with his tricks.

Now here he was again. Niagara he had crossed the ocean to walk once more. He had to do it, though he didn't exactly know why. It wasn't that he particularly wanted to any more, because it was true that he was old and tired now – perhaps was losing his skill. But it was there, and would remain there as long as he could put one foot forward on to a tightrope. And this one time now, with the wire at its new and impossibly dizzy height, was the most important moment in his life. This time was different from all the occasions in the past. Only Blondin knew. There would be no tricks this time. He was done with crowds. The cheers no longer mattered. He'd had those all his life as long as he could remember. This time there was just Blondin and his wire, higher than ever before, higher than even he had imagined. The waters seemed further and deeper than he had ever known, yet so near, and for almost the first time in his life, so easy to fall into. He looked at the wire and was afraid. The terrible drop between the wire and the deeps below was a gap he could feel. Never had he thought to know this within himself. Others had spoken of it before climbing to their wires and trapezes, but not Blondin.

As he looked, his past triumphs seemed to melt away. Nothing he'd done before mattered any longer, and to make things worse, he no longer knew if he could make it across his wire this time. He thought about the things he might do instead. Change his act altogether, perhaps, or just stop, give up, retire, unsurpassed in the eyes of the world. He'd earned a rest, and he'd made enough money in his performing life to live comfortably for the rest of it. But somehow he couldn't do that yet. This was the only real thing left to him, and he just had to get across for the last time. It wasn't simply that the wire was higher than ever before, nor that the Falls seemed so impossibly long down. He had to conquer the gap that filled his mind and made him tremble, so that his knees wouldn't stop jumping of their own accord, and his toes twitched on the red carpet with which they had paved his way to the wire.

The crowd had grown bigger than ever. Someone had spread the story that this was to be the last time: Blondin's swan-song. He'd never perform again, whether he crossed the wire or not. They whispered that it was all or nothing with him, and waited impatiently for something to happen. They had come from all over the countryside, people who had heard of this man, had not believed, had laughed incredulously, and now had come to see for themselves. Most of them had never set foot on a wire, had never climbed higher than the fencing which surrounded their chicken-runs at home. But there were, too, those who had dreamed of the high-wire in moments of time, and who regretted never having tested its strength with their own. They had come to see and experience at secondhand the thrills they had missed. There were the sceptics who had come to see him fall; the simple who came to be entertained. Finally there were the old 'Pros', his brothers in the art, who had walked the tightrope themselves, and now had come to watch with wise eyes the performance of their acknowledged master. These were the ones who walked the wire with him, who knew the taste in his mouth and the tightness of his throat. They would have held his hands and helped him over if they could, but they knew the aloneness, that it could be no other than it was. Besides, this was higher than any of them had ever reached; they had retired before Niagara.

Blondin walked up to where the thin silver wire stretched away from him over the emptiness beneath and the deeps below. Then he walked on further along the cliff top to look over into this great abyss. He saw the boiling crashing waters far, far below him. They thrashed and beat on the tumbled rocks at the bottom, and broke into white foaming fragments. Everything was confused and half-hidden by the glittering spray which shot back up from the shattering.

The crowd gasped. How could he bear to look? Everybody knew that heights were all right as long as you never looked down. It wasn't good to know how steep the drop, how terrible the fall, the crash at the bottom. It was better to keep your eyes fixed ahead, to look up even. Only then could you keep your

mind empty of the drop. Not to know what lay beneath was the only possible way to succeed.

But Blondin knew what waited for him down there. He had seen it before, though never so clearly as now – and it had filled his mind for years. Now he leaned far out over the edge to stare, only confirming what he had always known. The broken rocks and crashing water, the steep drop through emptiness, the gap between here and there, were more real in his mind than in his eyes as he looked.

He got up from where he had been hanging over the edge. Better get on with it. He felt a little stiff from the wetness of the air around him, and his knees cracked from the cold damp of the earth. It wasn't a good day. Indeed his manager, on arriving at the site, had strongly urged him not to attempt the crossing that day; to come back tomorrow, the next day, any day – so long as it was calm and still. But for Blondin it was the only day. As he waited he knew that the time had come. This was the right day for him, and he couldn't wait any longer.

He was not unduly troubled by the clouds that hung low and grey in the sky, nor by the coldness in his joints. A thin mist had gathered above the Falls, and in the middle swallowed up the wire so that it seemed not to be there. The thin wire, stretched so tight and high, reached out into nothingness: stopped in mid-air. He could see no end, and it seemed too, that to walk into invisibility might result in his stepping into the gap. 'Don't go. Don't go,' his manager urged. 'Of course, it's a pity to disappoint the crowd, but they'll come back. They always do. Anything for a thrill.' Privately, the crowd was thinking not of the walk, but of a fall. They felt a strange tension as the thought of tragedy touched them. They became restless with suppressed excitement and anticipation. Now they were urging a decision one way or the other. Some, like the manager, urged prudence, another day. Others, unwilling to be cheated of the spectacle, shouted at Blondin to 'Get on with it!'

The manager, wrapped up fatly in his great coat with the tight belt and fur collar, so enveloped he could scarcely move his arms, felt strongly about risking his prize exhibit. This was his livelihood after all, and had he not the right to grow fatter yet on Blondin's back? Yet still Blondin knew. Here was now, and he must go over or never. It worried him a little that the wire disappeared, that the opposite cliff was invisible. Worse still was the wind. It wasn't felt all the time, but blew spasmodically in sharp gusts which opened coats and snatched hats. It could be nasty, he thought, to meet that halfway across. It could upset the poise, whip up the ends of his pole on which he relied so strongly to retain his balance. The pole itself could become a danger. Still, he knew the wire was there, had seen it glinting in the sun the day before, thin and fine, but securely fixed and there all the way over. Now it hummed slightly, and sang into the wind. He felt a deep fondness for his wire warming him. He longed to be nothing else than he was. He would go. Nobody should stop him. The crowd was unimportant. He was alone. Blondin and his wire. The chaotic waters beneath, most of all that long gap, were his. Not even the thought of his manager, anxiously puffing out clouds of steam and stamping his feet, could make any difference. He liked him well enough. Jolly fellow, and a great help on the business side, the organisation, the money. He'd set the whole thing up out there. But well – he wasn't walking. It wasn't his wire.

Blondin stretched out his hand for the pole that would help him in his walk. It was thin and long and undulating as he grasped it firmly in both hands stretched out before him. He was ready to walk. He set his foot on the wire, bouncing it up and down to get the mood of it, to accustom his feet to its familiar feel. It was all right: firm, tense, and there all the way. The crowd was disappointed he didn't turn and wave. They would have liked to cheer. Poor showmanship. Things like that looked bad in a public performer. They did not know, how could they, that for Blondin they simply were not there. He had begun what he came for. Now there was only the wire, the broken deep below, the space between – together with the cold wind inside. He must reach the other side, and he would.

He took his first step forward. The wire began to move and sway beneath him as it always did. He was used to that. He bobbed and balanced as he stood there. The wind still troubled him. A cold eddy took the ends of the pole and whipped them up and down in its breath. Dangerous. Better to be rid of it now than be clinging on at the wrong moment. The pole fell silently, slowly, swiftly down. There was an exclamation from the crowd. The fat manager let out a strangled scream which was lost in the thunder of the waters. Blondin didn't hear. He felt better without the pole. Now it was really just him. He would do better than he thought: be more alone than he had imagined. He stretched out his arms rigidly on each side, looked straight and firm across to the invisible other side, and slowly at first, then almost trippingly, set out.

His feet slid their way along the wire, smoothly feeling out their path. He was light and could have danced. It didn't matter, he told himself, that he couldn't see the wire further on. His feet could feel it and that was all that mattered. In any case, maybe the mist would clear before he got there. It might not even cover much of the wire, and he would soon be through. He went on forward.

Now he was approaching the mist. His feet continued, but the grey folds were cold and wet. It was a sheet thrown over his head to confuse and hamper his movements. Yet still he was all right. He knew his wire and trusted his feet. His arms swayed each side of him like twin vanes. But now the wire began to twitch and sway treacherously. A wind inside the fog swirled it around him, hanging damp obscure folds over him, baffling his senses as it closed tighter on him. He couldn't go on. The wind and fog were too strong against him. Into his mind came the thought of turning back whilst he still could. Perhaps it would be wiser after all. No one would blame him under conditions like these. They'd even cheer, probably. 'Never mind, Blondin, you'll do it yet.' He saw the droop of his moustache as he stepped on to firm land, felt the shame in his eyes. The crowd parted to let him through, comforting him as he passed. Their respect for his earlier triumphs would be unimpaired. For Blondin it was the feeling of defeat. It was there, then gone. Blondin felt no more. He knew there was no going back. To turn in the fog and wind was impossible.

His mind was a stone. His feet were numb and unfeeling on the wire. It was dark, and he couldn't go forward. He twitched and swayed with the wire in the effort to retain his precarious balance. Only that unfelt determination kept him upright. Not even the long gap was in his mind, though somewhere deep was the knowledge that if he had to fall he would. Better that than go back. Blondin stood and waited. He was high over nothing, hidden by fog in the middle of his wire. In his mind he was in the water below, broken on the rocks. He had fallen through the gap.

On the side from which he had started the crowd had watched him disappear. A few drifted away, knowing they would not see him arrive at the other side. They were cold for their homes and firesides. The rest remained, waiting around for something they didn't know what. Though the far cliff was invisible, someone, they were sure, would send word what had happened. Maybe the cheers would echo back from the other side. In any case, you couldn't just leave someone out on a limb like that. No, better stay and see.

On the far side the expectant unknowing crowd stared hard with reddening eyes and cold hands. They tried to peer into the heart of the fog, hoping to see a small wraith emerging towards them. They strained to see, and it seemed a long time. There was nothing there yet. They looked at watches and knew that it was taking too long. It was getting late. Either he hadn't started (and you couldn't blame him really; it was a foul day), or . . . Just then the message filtered through that Blondin was on his way. They stretched their eyes further into the swirling fog which seemed at moments to part, only to come together again more impenetrably than before. There was nothing there. The wind was trying, perhaps, to blow away the clouds, but it would certainly blow away Blondin too, if it hadn't already.

The long silent minutes ticked by. They began to be afraid: to fear for Blondin, that something had happened to him. He couldn't come now. No one, not even the Maestro, could hang that long in air. It was all over. Yet they hadn't heard a cry. Maybe the wind had blown it back to the other side, or the noise of the waters drowned it. The fear that the worst had happened grew. No eyes met, though they no longer looked out from their end of the wire. The crowd was restless. They didn't know what to do. No one spoke, except the children who still expected the great man to appear at any moment and couldn't understand why there were tears in the grown-up eyes. 'When's he coming, Papa?' 'Mama, where is he?' 'Come on Blondin!' 'We want Blondin!' Their parents hushed them from above. It was all a bit puzzling. Perhaps he wasn't coming today after all. Perhaps he'd turned back. They hoped not, because they loved Blondin, the pictures and photographs they had seen of the funny little man. Well, it was hard luck, but he'd come some day they believed. Even if it could not be Blondin there were other men with wires and poles. They, better than the grown-ups, knew the problems. For hadn't they, many of them, practised on the wire fences around the place? They'd had some bangs and bruises, even broken arms and legs, at which their parents had drawn the line and forbidden such dangerous games. Still there were a few who secretly went on practising, and could not give up until the day when they too would be walking over Niagara. But the parents knew that Blondin had fallen, had failed, was by now dead. And they could not bring themselves to tell their children.

Blondin on the wire stood. And he stood, and he stood. And the cold stone in his mind sank as the wind parted the fog and whipped up the cold folds from his shoulders. A thin silver thread stretched once more in front of him. His feet began to move forward of their own accord, lightly and calmly. Blondin, arms straight out, head high, walked forward again, unseeing to the other side.

The crowd who had stopped looking, who despaired, saw a grey shadow. It couldn't be! It was! No! It wasn't possible! He must have gone down by this time! – But yes! It was, it really was! He was coming! He was through! A great cheer began, but was broken before it hit the air. He hadn't actually arrived yet, had he? Plenty could happen between here and there. Many a slip and all. The slightest mistake at any moment on the wire slippery with wetness, and the wind even stronger now, could cause disaster. But he was coming – and fast too. Heavens, the man was mad! He was actually running! He wasn't down. Here he came. There was a gasp of horror as his arms swirled wildly. He was nearly with them now. He was going to do it. They couldn't believe it, but were immeasurably glad. Hands reached out ready to grasp him. He'd made it. He'd arrived. He was here.

A great cheer, unchecked this time, welcomed him. 'Blondin! Blondin! Hurrah! Hurrah!' And Blondin, cold and wet from the water which had splashed him, and the dampness which had soaked beneath his skin, stood weary and exhausted on land again. Firm wet brown and green land stretched either side of the second red carpet. He'd done it. He looked back. The mist had lifted, blown up on the wind. The thin silver line stretched all the way back to the other side. He could see the crowd there leaping and waving – cheering too, no doubt. Blondin smiled. He smiled a smile that was weary, but happy and wise too, because he'd crossed the tightrope, and knew that never again would he have to fall into the abyss, the waters.

As he looked he saw what he had never seen before, the bridge that spanned the waterfall. It shone and glowed in all its colours. The spray glittered and was transformed in the light. It arced over the churning below, complete from side to side. Curious. It was always there. He'd just never noticed it before.

Acknowledgements

The Estate of P. L. Travers for 'Chapter 4: Topsy Turvy' from *Mary Poppins Comes Back* copyright © P. L. Travers 1935, first published by Peter Davies in 1935; Michael Morpurgo for 'The Silver Swan' copyright © Michael Morpurgo 2000, first published by Doubleday, a division of Penguin Random House in 2000; 'Secrets' from *Guardian Angels* copyright © Anita Desai 1987, first published by Viking Kestrel in 1987; Ann Pilling and Gina Pollinger for 'The Old Stone Faces' from *Mists and Magic* copyright © Ann Pilling 1983, first published by Lutterworth/Fonatana, 1983; Sally Christie for *Fishing with Dicky* copyright © Sally Christie 1992, first published by HarperCollins Young Lions in 1992; Alexander McCall Smith for 'Children of Wax' from *Children of Wax* copyright © Alexander McCall Smith 1987, first published by Canongate in 1987; 'The Snag' from *Tales of the Early World* copyright © Ted Hughes, first published by Faber & Faber Ltd; 'Hey, Danny!' from *Ratbags and Rascals* copyright © Robin Klein; Michael Rosen and the English and Media Centre for 'The Bakerloo Flea' from *Teachers' Writing*; Pauline Hill for 'Storm Children' from *Mists and Magic* copyright © Pauline Hill 1983, first

A classic collection of tales to tell children of about four, featuring beloved characters and lively stories, by Michael Bond, Jill Barklem and Anne Fine amongst others, chosen by children's book expert Julia Eccleshare.

Paddington Bear has a magical moment, the animals of Brambly Hedge are struggling at Dusty's mill, Lara's godmother sorts out a noisy lion and Rapunzel is rescued from the tower . . .

A classic collection of tales for young readers of about five, featuring beloved characters and lively stories by Michael Bond, Jill Barklem, Elizabeth Laird and others, chosen by children's book expert Julia Eccleshare.

Paddington Bear tries to buy a birthday present, the animals of Brambly Hedge set off to the seaside, a greedy queen insists on having the biggest tree in the world and will Cinderella get to go to the ball?

A classic collection of tales for young readers of about six, featuring beloved characters and lively stories by P. L. Travers, Jill Barklem, Michael Morpurgo and others, chosen by children's book expert Julia Eccleshare.

The Banks family are searching for a nanny, Macaw the parrot helps out at the fish and chip shop and a stonecutter dreams of becoming an emperor . . .

A classic collection of stories by P. L. Travers, Penelope Lively, Michael Morpurgo, Michael Rosen, Alexander McCall Smith and others, specially chosen for young readers of around seven by children's book expert Julia Eccleshare.

Mary Poppins takes Jane and Michael on a gravity-defying tea party on the ceiling, meet the boy who rescues a beached dolphin and can the barber keep the secret of the rajah's big ears?